TWEEDLEDUM AND TWEEDLEDEE

WILLOW ROSE

BOOKS BY THE AUTHOR

HARRY HUNTER MYSTERY SERIES

- ALL THE GOOD GIRLS
- RUN GIRL RUN
- NO OTHER WAY
- NEVER WALK ALONE

MARY MILLS MYSTERY SERIES

- WHAT HURTS THE MOST
- YOU CAN RUN
- YOU CAN'T HIDE
- CAREFUL LITTLE EYES

EVA RAE THOMAS MYSTERY SERIES

- DON'T LIE TO ME
- WHAT YOU DID
- NEVER EVER
- SAY YOU LOVE ME
- LET ME GO
- IT'S NOT OVER
- TO DIE FOR

EMMA FROST SERIES

- ITSY BITSY SPIDER
- MISS DOLLY HAD A DOLLY
- RUN, RUN AS FAST AS YOU CAN

- CROSS YOUR HEART AND HOPE TO DIE
- PEEK-A-BOO I SEE YOU
- TWEEDLEDUM AND TWEEDLEDEE
- EASY AS ONE, TWO, THREE
- THERE'S NO PLACE LIKE HOME
- SLENDERMAN
- WHERE THE WILD ROSES GROW
- WALTZING MATHILDA
- DRIP DROP DEAD
- BLACK FROST

JACK RYDER SERIES

- HIT THE ROAD JACK
- SLIP OUT THE BACK JACK
- THE HOUSE THAT JACK BUILT
- BLACK JACK
- GIRL NEXT DOOR
- HER FINAL WORD
- DON'T TELL

REBEKKA FRANCK SERIES

- ONE, TWO...HE IS COMING FOR YOU
- THREE, FOUR...BETTER LOCK YOUR DOOR
- FIVE, SIX...GRAB YOUR CRUCIFIX
- SEVEN, EIGHT...GONNA STAY UP LATE
- NINE, TEN...NEVER SLEEP AGAIN
- ELEVEN, TWELVE...DIG AND DELVE
- THIRTEEN, FOURTEEN...LITTLE BOY UNSEEN
- BETTER NOT CRY
- TEN LITTLE GIRLS
- IT ENDS HERE

MYSTERY/THRILLER/HORROR NOVELS

- In One Fell Swoop
- Umbrella Man
- Blackbird Fly
- To Hell in a Handbasket
- Edwina

HORROR SHORT-STORIES

- Mommy Dearest
- The Bird
- Better watch out
- Eenie, Meenie
- Rock-a-Bye Baby
- Nibble, Nibble, Crunch
- Humpty Dumpty
- Chain Letter

PARANORMAL SUSPENSE/ROMANCE NOVELS

- In Cold Blood
- The Surge
- Girl Divided

THE VAMPIRES OF SHADOW HILLS SERIES

- Flesh and Blood

- Blood and Fire
- Fire and Beauty
- Beauty and Beasts
- Beasts and Magic
- Magic and Witchcraft
- Witchcraft and War
- War and Order
- Order and Chaos
- Chaos and Courage

THE AFTERLIFE SERIES

- Beyond
- Serenity
- Endurance
- Courageous

THE WOLFBOY CHRONICLES

- A Gypsy Song
- I am WOLF

DAUGHTERS OF THE JAGUAR

- Savage
- Broken

Tweedledum and Tweedledee
  Agreed to have a battle;
  For Tweedledum said Tweedledee
  Had spoiled his nice new rattle.

Just then flew down a monstrous crow,
  As black as a tar-barrel;
  Which frightened both the heroes so,
  They quite forgot their quarrel.

ENGLISH NURSERY RHYME

PROLOGUE
APRIL 2014

The man followed the family closely with his eyes. Far behind him, the big city of Rome lay enthroned with its ancient buildings and ruins...This great city of gladiators, lunatic drivers and sumptuous pasta dishes. They had left behind the Vespas, nippy little Fiats and red sports cars speeding past trendy sidewalk bistros, tourists rushing to climb the famous Spanish Steps, walking through the Piazza Navona or tossing a coin into the Trevi Fountain. In front of them was the harbor...the cruise terminals at Civitavecchia, outside of town.

The sun was about to set out on the water behind *The Crystal Bliss*. The man stayed close to the family. He studied the father, whom he knew was a doctor, meticulously as he put his arm around the shoulder of his daughter. They were smiling while they walked onboard the ship, not noticing the strange man following their every move.

"This is going to be great, isn't it?" the man heard the doctor say to his wife. The wife smiled and nodded.

The man walking behind the family smiled too. He had waited for this moment, for this chance while carrying his heavy pain on his shoulder.

They walked up towards the entrance of the grandiose ship and the family stopped for a second to look at the ancient city in the far distance and the ruins in whose name the Caesars sought to claim the world.

"See you in two weeks," the doctor said and saluted the city.

Then he laughed.

"Dad, you're so theatrical," the daughter exclaimed.

They walked inside. The man followed them, leaving a few people between them. He was warm in his big coat and hat. He was sweating heavily. The couple behind him were fighting. A child accidentally pushed his arm. The man growled in pain and looked down at the child.

"Sorry, sir," the child said, slightly shivering once his eyes met those of the man. The child let out a small shriek. Then he pulled back and waited for his mother to catch up with him.

"Mom, that man has a hunchback," the man heard the boy say to his mother. "Like Quasimodo."

The mother hushed the boy. "It's not nice to say things like that."

The man didn't care what the boy said. He rushed towards the entrance of the ship and followed the family closely till they reached their suite on the penthouse deck. He watched them walk inside and stayed until the door closed behind them.

The man remembered the number on the door, then turned and walked down the stairs towards his own cabin.

Moving bodies surrounded him, smiling mouths, with words being exchanged among them. In the distance, there was music playing. Strings were giving the ship a pleasant ambiance, giving the passengers the feeling of luxury that they had paid for.

The man walked down the stairs, carrying his heavy suitcase in his left hand. He found his small cabin on the lower deck. It had no windows, but the man liked it that way. The solitude and the noise from the ship's engine were both perfect for his purpose.

He closed the door and put his suitcase on the floor next to the bed. He was sweating and took off his hat, then his big coat. He looked at the reflection in the mirror in the small bathroom. The voice filled the room.

"Finally. I feel so lonely when kept in the dark."

"You'll never be alone again, Deedee. Never again."

1

APRIL 1970

It was the happiest day in the lives of Mr. and Mrs. Rosetti. The day they were going to have their baby.

It happened on a Monday and Mr. Rosetti had already left for his job at the railway station at *Roma Termini* when his wife went into labor. He was walking across the *Piazza dei Cinquecento*, in the heart of the city when his good colleague Piero came running towards him from the proud building that contained the central station of Rome and had done so since it was constructed in 1867.

"Salvatore, Salvatore," Piero yelled.

"What's going on?" Salvatore Rosetti asked, startled.

Piero caught his breath. "It's your wife. She's in labor. You better hurry to the hospital. They called less than five minutes ago."

Salvatore felt a dizziness. He could hardly believe his ears. Was this it? Was this finally it? There were still three days till she was due.

Piero smiled and put his hand on Salvatore's shoulder. He laughed. "It is happening, Salvatore. You are going to be a father, you lucky bastard. Now come with me. You can take my Vespa."

Salvatore rushed through Rome's heavy morning traffic, thinking of nothing but how his life was about to change. For the better, of course. That's what they said, wasn't it?

Your life will never be the same again. Once a father, always a father.

Yes, that was what he had been looking forward to for the past many months. He was young...only twenty-one, but knew he was ready to become a father.

Salvatore parked the Vespa in front of the hospital and stormed inside. A nurse told him to wait in the waiting area till the doctor came out. His wife was still in labor, they said. No baby yet.

Salvatore nodded humbly and sat down in a chair in the waiting room where another expectant father was waiting impatiently and anxiously. He was sweating and walked around restlessly. The two of them shook hands.

"My brother's wife had complications," the other man said. "They told him there was nothing they could do. That's why I'm nervous. Most of the time, it goes perfectly well, but sometimes...well sometimes, things simply go wrong."

Salvatore nodded. He had never thought of the possibility that something could go wrong. It was, after all, something that happened every day all over the world, wasn't it? It was the most natural thing in the world.

Finally, the door to the room opened and a doctor showed up. He looked at both of them with a serious expression.

"Signor Moretti?"

The other man in the waiting room looked anxiously at the doctor. "That's me. Is she alright?"

Finally, the doctor smiled. "She's fine. They're both fine. You had a baby girl."

The man roared with joy. "A girl!" He turned and looked at Salvatore with a victorious expression. "Did you hear that? It's a girl. It's a girl!"

"*Felicitazioni*," the doctor said. Then he turned around and left the room.

Salvatore felt a huge lump in his throat.

"Congratulations," he said to the man who was still cheering loudly.

"I'm a father. I'm a father! I can't believe it. And you will be soon too. We will both be fathers. Ha ha ha. This is amazing. I tell you."

Salvatore nodded with his head bent. He had no idea how long this would take. He stared at the door the doctor had gone through, while biting his lip. His hands were getting sweaty. He got up and walked to the window and looked out at the many people transporting themselves from one place to another. Happy smiling faces from people going to work or tourists exploring his great city. Meanwhile, he was hearing his older brother's voice in his mind.

Your life will never be the same.

Finally, the door opened and another doctor came in. His expression was as serious as the first one had been. It didn't have to mean anything, did it?

"Signor Rosetti," the doctor said.

"That's me," Salvatore stuttered.

"I'm afraid I have some bad news."

Salvatore's heart stopped. His hands were shaking. "Bad news? What kind of bad news?"

Please, oh God. Please!

"There were complications. Your wife...well we didn't know..."

"My wife what? What didn't you know?"

"There was more than one. You had twins. Unfortunately, they're what we call conjoined."

"Conjoined? What does that mean?" Salvatore asked, confused.

"Conjoined twins are identical twins that have been joined in utero," the doctor said. "Some people call them Siamese twins."

"I...I don't understand."

"Their two bodies are fused at the abdomen and pelvis. Other than that, they're in perfect condition. They are boys."

"But...Giulia?"

"I'm afraid she didn't make it. There were...complications. She lost too much blood." The doctor drew in a deep breath, then put his hand on Salvatore's shoulder. A nurse appeared behind him.

"Ah, there they are," the doctor said. He grabbed the small wrapped bundle that the nurse was holding and handed it to Salvatore. "There you go. Say hello to your sons."

Salvatore looked down at the two babies wrapped in a white blanket. The nurse next to him forced a smile. The doctor cleared his throat.

"Congratulations."

Then he turned around and left. The nurse gave Salvatore another of her pitiful smiles, then followed close behind the doctor. Salvatore removed the blanket and gasped when he saw the two faces joined in one body. The babies' eyes were open and they looked up at him. Salvatore cried and shook his head. He remembered having seen people like this as a child when he went to the big circus that always set up outside of town in the spring. Freaks. That's what they were. That's what people called them.

Salvatore walked down the hallway of the hospital with heavy burdened steps and continued out into the street, carrying his sons in his arms.

That's what they call them. They'll call them freaks.

Salvatore walked across the street and blended into the crowd. In a state of pure shock, he walked without knowing where to go. He didn't notice the faces of the people he passed on his way, he didn't hear their voices. All he could sense was his own heartbeat and his many thoughts. He felt like crying for the loss of Guilia and the future he thought they would spend together. He didn't even look at the small faces in the bundle he was carrying. He didn't want to look at them.

They'll be nothing but a disgrace to you and your family.

Salvatore walked for what could have been hours with the crying babies in his arms, hearing nothing but his mother's voice in his mind.

I told you not to marry that woman, Salvatore. I knew she would get you in trouble. Didn't I tell you so? Didn't I?

Salvatore walked past an alley and finally stopped. He turned and walked into the alley. Tears were rolling heavily across his cheeks as he came closer to the dumpster.

I know I'm going to Hell for this. Forgive me, Father. Forgive me!

He opened the lid and carefully placed the babies on top of the garbage, then closed the lid and shut out their cries.

Then he ran. Ran for his life.

2

APRIL 2014

"We're going on a cruise. I can't wait!"

My mother laughed and turned to look at me. We were sitting in a taxi-bus, going from Rome to the cruise-ship terminals outside of town. We had left our island the same morning and flown there from Copenhagen.

"Oh come on. Cheer up," she said and gave me an elbow in the side. "Maya is with her father. She'll be fine."

"I know. I just miss her. That's all. She's been living with her father for a month now and I can't stand it. I miss her."

My mother nodded. Her face was still scarred heavily from the hot coffee that had been thrown in her face two months ago. But somehow, I thought she looked better this way. At least she looked real. The doctors had taken skin from her thigh and put it on her face and, to be honest, they had done a really good job. She had been depressed about it for a couple of weeks after the incident, so my dad had decided to take all of us on a cruise for Easter. I guess he hoped it would cheer her up a little.

Victor had ten days off from school. The cruise was twelve days, so I had taken him out for a couple more days. The school told me they didn't mind. I guess they still had their trouble with him. I had gotten a lot of help the past few weeks from Ole Knudsen, who had started working with Victor, but even he found it hard to really get inside of Victor and know what was going on. He was going to continue trying, but he told me it might take a long time.

"When are we there?" Sophia's oldest son Christoffer asked.

I had brought him on the trip with us. Since Maya didn't want to come, I had given him her ticket. I thought it would be good for Victor to have someone else there with him. To have another child to hang out with. Christoffer was almost two years older than Victor and a really sweet boy. I thought he might be able to somehow get Victor out of his shell.

"I know you miss Maya. But she needs her space right now," my mother said. "It's a lot for her to take in. Let her go for a little while and she'll be back before you know it. You're her mother and that will never change."

"I just hope Michael is treating her well. He wasn't exactly thrilled about the thought of her living with him all of a sudden. Especially not after I told him the truth. He is still angry with me and suddenly saw no reason why he should have Maya living with him if he *wasn't even her real father*. It broke my heart that he could feel that way. He is the only father Maya has ever known. I really wanted her to come on this cruise with us, but she doesn't even want to talk to me. I just hope she's alright, you know? I mean she had to start a new school and everything. It's a lot for her right now."

"Maya will be fine," my dad said. "She's a big girl. And we're going to have a great time on this cruise, aren't we Victor?"

Victor was sitting next to him on the mini-bus. He didn't answer, but kept staring out the window. He hadn't been doing very well ever since the bank incident and I was very worried about him. He hardly spoke anymore to any of us and he was more closed up than ever. It was like he chose to stay in his own world because it was safer. I couldn't blame him. Every now and then, I wished I could simply disappear into a world of my own as well. Especially when I was around my mom and dad lately. I was thrilled that they were back together and trying to make it work. That was truly amazing, but they had started acting like teenagers in love and it was getting slightly nauseating. They were constantly kissing and touching each other, my mom sitting on my dad's lap, giggling like a schoolgirl. It was sweet in the beginning, but now I was kind of getting tired of it.

It was nice to get out of the house, though, and I was glad my dad invited us along. I would have liked to bring Morten as well, but he couldn't get the time off from the police station. Part of me felt that he wasn't too eager to go anyway, so I didn't push for him to come. It wasn't that he didn't want to be with me and my family, but he told me he didn't like sailing that much. He got seasick really easily and he didn't like the idea of being in the middle of the Mediterranean Sea without being able to get to land when he wanted to. It was too claustrophobic for him.

"I, for one, can't wait to see our suite onboard," my dad said and looked lovingly at my mom.

She giggled. "Oh Bengt. You're so naughty."

"How's that naughty?" I asked annoyed. "I'm looking forward to seeing my suite as well."

My mother shrugged. "Well you know..."

"Thank you. I don't want to know. I want to enjoy my vacation without thinking about what the two of you are doing in there."

The taxi-bus stopped and the driver told us we had arrived. I looked out the window and saw the enormous ship anchored at the quay. I don't think I'd ever seen anything like it.

"Wow," I exclaimed.

"I know," my dad said. "Isn't she a beauty? The Crystal Bliss known quite simply as the very best cruise ship in the world. It has won several awards for its luxury. Celebrities from all over Europe travel on this baby."

"This must have been expensive, Dad?" I asked, as we got out of the mini-bus and I could see the ship's complete size. It was a beauty.

"Well nothing but the best for the people I love, right?" he said.

3

APRIL 2014

M y dad had gotten us penthouse suites. I could hardly believe my eyes when I realized it. It was quite overwhelming. I knew the price for one of those was around twelve thousand Euros. I couldn't believe my dad had paid that much. I guess he was just happy to have my mother back and wanted her to know it. He wanted her to never miss Pedro or the life she led in Spain again. And my dad had a lot of money. He still had his dental clinic outside of Copenhagen and he did very well as far as I knew. Plus, he did a little extra on the side. There was a great need for dentists, since there was only one on the island and he needed all the help he could get. So the local dentist had contacted my dad once he learned that he had moved there and asked him if he could help out a little with the acute patients. It wasn't for the money, but it kept him busy and he loved helping people out. That's why he went into the dental business in the first place, he kept telling me.

A cabin-boy showed us to our suite where we were going to spend the next twelve days. He smiled when he unlocked the door and saw the expression on my face. The view was...I wanted to say spectacular, but that somehow wasn't enough.

"Magnifico, si?" the cabin-boy said, with his cute very white smile.

Victor was hiding behind me. Christoffer walked right in like he owned the place. "Wow," he exclaimed. "This is nice!"

"That it sure is," I said and walked towards the big windows with views of the ocean reaching as far as I could see. The sun was about to set and painted the sky in many different tones of orange. The cabin-boy put my suitcase down in the entrance. I gave him a tip and he left. Victor walked across the light carpet. He stopped in front of something hanging on the wall above the mini-bar. I chuckled. The fire axe. Of course that was something he'd like to look at. The expensive suite with the great view and art on the walls didn't matter much, but the axe fascinated him. I continued through the glass doors into the living room.

"Oh my. There is a huge flat screen TV in here, Vic. And a great couch." I sat down and felt the sofa. It was perfect. I sank right into it. I chuckled as I threw a glance around the living room. I told Christoffer the small bedroom to the right was his. Victor and I were going to sleep together in the master bedroom. That way, Christoffer could have some privacy when he wanted it. He found his bed and threw his suitcase on it.

"I could get used to living like this, what do you say Victor? It's really nice, huh? And look at the view. We're on the top floor of the ship, buddy. We can see everything from here. And there's a balcony. We can sit out here and eat if we want to. Order food to our room and enjoy it out here while we sail across the Mediterranean Sea. You know we're going all the way to Istanbul in Turkey, right?"

He didn't answer. I knew he wouldn't. But it was okay. I knew he heard me. I smiled and looked at him. He hadn't spoken at all to Christoffer on the trip here. Maybe it was a bad idea, after all, to bring someone else. Maybe Victor really needed my attention and some alone-time with his mother. Well, I couldn't change it now. Besides, I enjoyed Christoffer's company.

Christoffer walked up next to me. He stared out the big windows. "Thank you so much for bringing me here," he said. "I've never been on a cruise before. I've actually never left the island before."

I smiled. "I know. You just enjoy it, okay?"

"Oh, I will."

"Good."

I looked at him and enjoyed the expression on his face. He was such a good boy. Having five children, Sophia never had the money to give him an experience like this. I was glad to be able to give it to him.

"How long is there till the ship leaves the quay?" Christoffer asked.

"Not long. Half an hour maybe?" I said.

"Please tell me when. I don't want to miss it. I think I'll have to catch up on some reading while we wait. My teacher told us to read Lewis Carroll's *Through the Looking-Glass*...you know, the story of Alice in Wonderland over Easter break, so I better get started."

"Of course. I'll let you know."

Christoffer smiled. He had a very pretty face. "Great. Thanks. And thanks again for bringing me here."

"No problem. Just enjoy."

"I definitely will."

Christoffer went into his bedroom and closed the door. He was so polite. To be frank, he was my favorite among Sophia's children. He was always taking care of his younger siblings. It was good for him to get treated a little for once.

Maya was going to be so jealous once I started posting pictures on Facebook of this place. She was going to regret saying no. At least I hoped she would. I picked up my phone and took a series of pictures of the suite and posted them right away. Victor still hadn't moved. I walked to him into the bedroom and sat next to him on the bed.

"Don't you want to go out on the balcony and have a look?" I asked.

He still didn't move.

I drew in a deep breath. "You miss her too, don't you? I guess we both do. But we'll have to get by for a little while without her. She'll be back. At least, I hope she will. Oh God, Victor. What if she doesn't come back?"

I paused. "No, you're right. Of course she will. We're her family. She'll be back. Of course she will."

I felt tears build up in my eyes, but refused to cry. "Look at your old mom, tearing up because her daughter is growing up, huh?" I sniffled and got up. The ship suddenly made a loud noise. "Did you hear that, buddy?

That's the horn. Do you think we're setting off to sea now? Come. Let's get out on the balcony."

I walked through the glass door. Victor followed me reluctantly. The ship started moving. I looked at Victor. "Do you want to go wave to people down at the quay? Yeah, let's do that. Come."

"Why?" Victor asked. "We don't know any of them."

"Let's do it anyway. It'll be fun."

"No it won't."

"Don't be so boring, Victor."

I knocked on the door to Christoffer's room.

"The ship is sailing now. We're going out to wave; do you want to come?"

Christoffer opened the door and jumped out. "I'd love to."

We walked fast towards the door. Victor followed me very closely. In the hallway, we met my mom and dad. They were holding hands and wearing big smiles.

"We're leaving now," my dad said.

"I know."

We followed the stream of people and entered a big deck with a huge pool area. Victor, Christoffer and I found a spot by the railing. Christoffer and I waved to the people down at the quay while the ship slowly maneuvered out of the port. Victor just stared at them, holding on tight to the railing.

"Wow," Christoffer exclaimed. "Look at how small the people are. And look at the view. I can see all of Rome in the distance. I've always wanted to see Rome. I would love to see the Colosseum."

I patted him on the head. "You will one day."

A man standing next to me on the other side was wearing a long coat and a hat. I found it strange, since it was still very hot outside.

"Cute boys you have there," he said. "How old are they?"

"Victor is eight," I said with a smile. "Turning nine next month. It's his first time on a cruise."

"He's big for an eight-year old, then," the man said.

"Well, we're Scandinavian. We're very tall. Well, except for me," I said and laughed.

The man didn't laugh. He stared at Victor. It felt a little uncomfortable.

"And the other one?"

"Christoffer is ten. It's his first time on a cruise too."

"Ah, ten is a wonderful age," the man said. "What a beautiful face."

I touched Christoffer's curly hair and pulled him closer. "Yes, he is a pretty boy. Going to crush a lot of hearts in a few years."

"Probably," the man said and lifted his hat gently. "Enjoy your cruise,"

I followed him with my eyes as he disappeared into the waving and cheering crowd. When I turned to look again, the quay and the people were nothing but a distant memory.

4

APRIL 2014

The man hurried down the stairs towards his cabin on the lower deck. He was running late. Deedee hated it when he was late.

The man opened the door and closed it behind him. He took off the coat and put it on a hanger.

"What took you so long?" the voice said.

"I'm sorry Deedee. But I was held up. I'm sorry."

Deedee snorted angrily.

"I brought you pasta. Linguine. You love Linguine," the man said.

Deedee growled. "Ai Frutti di Mare?"

"Just the way you like it. And I brought you wine."

Finally, Deedee was content. They ate in deep silence. The man was sweating and had hardly any appetite.

"I think you're coming down with a fever," Deedee said. "You're burning up."

"I know," the man said and wiped sweat off his forehead. "It's just the infection in the wound. It's nothing. I have antibiotics. It'll be fine. Don't worry."

"I don't," Deedee said. "I can't worry about you. I have enough of worries of my own."

"You shouldn't have to worry," the man said. "I'm taking good care of you. I promised I would, remember? I'm going to make everything good again. I won't let you down. I promise."

The man groaned in pain, found a bottle of pills in his pocket and took one, washing it down with wine. He closed his eyes and leaned back. The wine helped take the edge off the pain. Soon, the pills would kick in as well. It was all going to be alright. A good night's sleep would do the trick. He had an important day ahead of him. He needed all of his strength.

"Don't fail me," Deedee hissed.

"I'm not. I'm just resting. Gathering strength." The man sipped his wine again and ate the rest of his pasta. He was feeling better already. The pasta and wine made him drowsy. It was a good sign. Maybe he would get some sleep tonight?

"I'm sad," Deedee growled.

"I know. I know," the man replied, trying to sound as compassionate as possible. "It won't be much longer now. Soon, it will all be much better. Just wait and see. Now we need to go to sleep."

The man undressed; all the while, his shoulder was throbbing. He turned off the light and, as his head hit the pillow and the darkness surrounded him, he felt the sorrows of his past once again flush in over him. He felt like crying, but didn't. He refused to feel sorry for himself. Instead he let the anger rise in him and fed off of it.

"You're thinking about it again," Deedee said. "I just know you are. It's going to keep you awake all night, and me as well. Stop thinking about it."

"I'm not," the man lied.

"Just go to sleep," Deedee said.

"I will."

The man tried to empty his mind and lie completely still, but still couldn't find rest. The discomfort in his body kept him awake, along with the sounds. There were many sounds on the ship at night. He hated this restlessness that he always felt. The feeling that everything was wrong. He loathed this endless grief that had taken such a stronghold in his mind and saddened his every thought.

"I'm gonna make it right. I promise you that, Deedee," he whispered into the darkness. "I promise it to you."

5

APRIL 1976

No one ever stopped reminding the twins that they had been found in a dumpster. At the orphanage where they were taken to after an old lady found them while throwing out her garbage, they reminded them every day.

"Garbage-boys, garbage-boys," the other children yelled after them.

Even the staff working there called them names. Mostly names like *circus freaks* and *monstrosities*. They had given them real names. When the lady had brought them to the home, they hadn't known whether it was one child or two. Should they give them one name or two? Finally, they had decided to name them after the twins from Alice in Wonderland.

Their names were Tweedledee and Tweedledum. Soon reduced to just Deedee and Dumdum.

At six years of age, Tweedledee and Tweedledum started to realize just how different they were from everyone else. Not just because the other children told them, but they noticed how people would gasp or shriek when they saw them in the street. They tried to leave the orphanage as little as possible to avoid the staring eyes, but life inside the orphanage was rough on the boys and often they needed to get out in order to avoid being beaten up constantly. Everyone picked on the freak-brothers and told them they belonged in a circus. And they were easy to beat up, since they still didn't know quite how to control their mutual body enough to be able to hit back. Between them, the boys only had three legs, two heads and four arms. They could stand up, but they couldn't walk and, instead, they would crawl on their hands and feet, making them look like a giant two-headed spider. They had learned to coordinate their arms enough to be able to eat. They had separate heads and brains, but still thought very alike. They liked the same things and often finished each other's sentences. They had even developed a language of their own between them, one only the two of them could understand. But they weren't allowed to use it, so they only did it when they were alone.

No one told them it was their six-year birthday, but the boys knew what month they had come to the orphanage and, therefore, decided on a date and on that day, they left the orphanage in the morning and didn't come back.

They had planned the trip for months. All of their life they had dreamt of one thing and that was to see the ocean. They had read about it in books and seen pictures in magazines at the orphanage. And they had both agreed. They had to see it. No matter the cost. It was like it was calling to them.

So, Tweedledee and Tweedledum stole a handful of cash from the daily leader of the orphanage, Mrs. Campari's purse when she wasn't in her office and used some to pay the bus to take them there.

The twins hadn't been prepared for the reaction of the other people on the bus. Their deep gasps and small whines surprised the twins as they crawled on their hands through the bus to find a seat. People put their bags and purses on the seats next to them to let them know they wouldn't sit next to a set of freaks like them.

Tweedledee and Tweedledum found a seat in the back and sat down quietly. The bus started up and drove into the street. The bus was quiet. No one uttered a word. A couple of children stared at the twins with open mouth and eyes. Their mother told them not to stare. The twins turned their heads and looked at each other. It was like looking into a mirror, except one was slightly bigger than the other.

"I love you," one brother whispered to the other in the language they only understood.

"I love you more," the other replied.

The bus stopped at the harbor and the twins got out. They could already smell the ocean in the distance and crawled fast across the street towards it, causing the traffic to come to a stop. They were laughing and quickly forgetting everything about staring looks and frowning faces. As their hands hit the sand, they took off their four flip-flops they wore on their hands, rolled up the trousers that had been sewn specially for them by Mrs. Telesca, who cooked for the children in the orphanage, to fit their three legs. Then they looked at each other quickly before storming into the ocean and getting their feet and legs wet.

They loved how the water felt against their skin. They played in it, splashed it at each other, and laughed heartily and happily for the first time in their short life.

The two brothers both looked into the other one's eyes and smiled. "We'll always have each other," they said simultaneously. "It doesn't matter about all these people. Not as long as we are together."

The twins danced on their hands in the water for a long time, getting all of their clothes soaking wet. Then, they crawled back up on the beach and sat down in the sand, staring at the endless ocean where a huge tanker was heading out to sea.

"Where do you think they are?" Tweedledee asked.

Tweedledum didn't have to get more details to understand that his brother meant their parents. They had been wondering all of their lives where they were.

"I think they're looking for us somewhere out there."

They both looked out at the ocean and simultaneously decided they didn't want to go back to the orphanage again. They barely finished the shared thought before they heard steps coming up behind them.

6

APRIL 2014

We arrived at Sorrento at eight in the morning. It was the first stop on our cruise. All night we had been sailing down the coast of Italy, but it was the first time I actually saw the magnificent coast. It was truly breathtaking.

I, for one, had slept excellently. When I woke up, I found Victor sitting in the living room reading a book.

"What are you reading?" I asked and looked at the cover. "Lewis Carroll's *Through the Looking-Glass?* You're reading Christoffer's book?" I shrugged. "Guess there's no harm in that."

I walked to the balcony and saw the city of Sorrento in front of me. The town was situated on a cliff overlooking the Bay of Naples. I had ordered breakfast in the room and ate it on the balcony with Victor and Christoffer, while studying the city online. Christoffer ate eagerly, while Victor, as usual, was more reluctant.

"Better eat some more, buddy," I said, when he was about to leave the table. "We have a long and busy day ahead of us. We're going to see Mount Vesuvius and the city of Pompeii. You remember what happened to it, right? We talked about it at home. They were all buried in ashes when the volcano erupted. It's still active, you know. I saw it ten years ago on a trip here. Smoke was coming out of the side of the volcano while I was walking on it."

"Wow," Christoffer said.

"I know. It's been like this for many years. But I want you both to remember that we have to walk all the way up there. It's a long walk and I want you to have the energy for it, okay? I think this will be something you'll enjoy, Victor."

"I'd like to see the dead people," Victor suddenly said. "The ones that show the positions they were in when they died."

I chuckled. "I bet you would. There are a few of them. You'll see them when we come to the city. Some look like they're screaming. They're not real bodies, you know."

"What are they then?" Christoffer asked.

I scrolled the text on my iPad. "It says here that *the objects that lay beneath the city were well preserved for centuries because of the lack of air and moisture. These artifacts provide an extraordinarily detailed insight into the life of a city during the Pax Romana. During the excavation, plaster was used to fill in the voids between the ash layers that once held human bodies. This allowed one to see the exact position the person was in when he or she died.* So it's more like a print of someone dying."

"Nasty," Christoffer exclaimed.

"I want to see it," Victor said and took another bite of the buttered bread I had made for him.

"I know you do."

I sipped my coffee, thinking any other mother might be concerned about her son's fascination with violent deaths, but not me. I was just happy that Victor was talking to me and that he had an interest to keep him in the same world as me. It was one of the few things we could actually talk about. So I let him have it. It was his thing.

"We might take a trip to the island of Capri if we have the time," I said. "There's a blue grotto there that I'd like to see. But it depends on how long the trip to Pompeii takes. I don't want to wear you out. We could do it tomorrow. The ship stays in this harbor until five o'clock tomorrow afternoon. So we have plenty of time."

A little later, there was a knock on my door and I went to open it. Outside stood my mom and dad. They were dressed like tourists with money belts and everything. They were both smiling widely while holding hands. Even my mother was smiling. I couldn't remember when I last saw her this happy.

"Are you guys ready?" My dad asked.

"Almost there," I said. "Come in."

"So how are you liking your suite?" my dad asked as they walked inside.

Victor was sitting on the bed. He had been ready to go for a long time. Christoffer was in the bathroom.

"I love it, Dad," I yelled while brushing my hair and putting on mascara at the same time. "But wasn't it kind of expensive?"

"It was. But you're worth it," my dad replied.

"You're so sweet Bengt," my mom said and kissed him.

I looked at myself in the mirror, then decided it had to be enough. I grabbed my purse and walked towards them. They were still kissing and rubbing their noses. Christoffer came out of the bathroom.

"You're the sweet one here," my dad said.

I cleared my throat. "We're ready."

7

APRIL 2014

Alberto Colombo had been awake all night. He had been playing in the casino onboard the ship and lost track of time. He hadn't noticed that it was morning already, since there were no windows or clocks in the casino to warn him to get back to the suite. His parents had planned a trip and told him they were leaving the ship early in the morning. But Alberto didn't want to go. He didn't care about seeing all those things. He had just turned fourteen, but had a fake ID to let anyone who cared enough to ask know that he was old enough.

He had snuck out of the suite the night before when his parents fell asleep. He had taken his mom's wallet and first he had won in blackjack, but then lost it all again after hours at the roulette wheel. It didn't matter. He had more money in his trust fund than he would ever be able to spend in his lifetime. He just wished he could get ahold of that money now and not have to wait till he turned eighteen.

Until then, he had to live with what his parents gave him. It was humiliating, he thought. To have to ask for money. Alberto sipped his cocktail that he had been served by one of the gorgeous waitress. He'd had a few too many of those during the night and had been drunk for the last couple of hours.

"Place your bets please," the dealer said.

Alberto placed the last of his money on red fifteen. A few seconds later, it landed on black twenty-two. Alberto laughed. How ridiculous. He had spent ten thousand Euros of his mother's money in just a few hours and she would never even notice. Just like she never noticed anything else Alberto did.

"Are you playing, sir?" The dealer asked.

Alberto shook his head. "No. Better get going."

Alberto walked slowly towards the exit. He was swaying and accidentally stumbled into some guy who grabbed him by the arm to make sure he didn't fall. Alberto laughed. "Wow, the ship is rocking huh?" he said and regained his balance.

"The ship docked half an hour ago," the man said.

Alberto's smile froze. "What did you say?"

"The ship is docked. We're in Sorrento."

"Shit." Alberto exclaimed. "Oh my God. My parents are going to kill me! I gotta get back!"

Alberto started running. He blasted the doors to the casino open and stormed out. The bright daylight hit him like a punch to his face and he squinted his eyes so he wouldn't be blinded. There were people everywhere...walking and chatting. There was music playing from the speakers. It all felt so confusing.

Up. Up. You have to get upstairs to your suite. Maybe they'll still be in there. Maybe they haven't left yet.

"Excuse me," Alberto said and fought his way through the crowd of people walking towards the exit to leave the ship. "Excuse me. Coming through. Sorry sir. Didn't mean to hit you. I'm just trying to get..."

Alberto used his elbows and finally managed to make his way to the elevator. But it took too long for it to arrive and he decided on the stairs instead. He stormed up while hundreds of people were making their way down. He reached the top floor and stormed down the corridor. He grabbed the door handle and tried to open the door to the suite he was sharing with his parents.

It's locked. Crap. And I left my phone in the suite.

Alberto knocked hard on the door. "Mama? Papa?"

No answer. A cabin-boy came towards him. "Can I help you, sir?"

"I locked myself out. I need to get something from inside the suite," Alberto said.

The cabin-boy blushed. "You're Alberto Colombo aren't you? Son of the famous race-driver Alonzo Colombo, right?"

Alberto sighed. He got this a lot. But this time it might be of help. "Yes. Yes I am. Could you please help me?"

"Naturally."

The cabin-boy stepped forward and slid his card through the reader. "There you go, Mr. Colombo."

"Thank you," Alberto said and stormed past him into the suite.

"Mom?" he yelled, but there was no answer. Her purse was gone.

Alberto found his own phone on the table beside his bed. Next to it was a note.

We left. You stay here and think about what you've done. Didn't you think I would find out if you spent ten thousand Euros from my credit card? They called from the bank. We'll find a proper punishment once we get back tonight. Your father isn't happy. Don't leave the room.

Alberto fell backwards onto the bed. This wasn't good. It was worse than the time he had taken one of his father's cars and drove into a light pole in the street. He could tell by the tone of his mother's note. But worst of all was the disappointment in Alberto's mind. He couldn't believe they had just left without him. Weren't they the least bit worried about him? Why hadn't they gone out to look for him?

Stay in the room, the note said. Alberto looked at the clock. His parents probably weren't going to be back until late in the afternoon. He had a choice now. He could stay and do as he was told and get punished. Or he could not. It didn't matter. He would still get punished either way. He looked at his mother's credit card.

Might as well have some fun while I have the chance.

Alberto got up from the bed and walked towards the door. If he was going to get punished no matter what, it might as well be for something really good.

8

APRIL 2014

He had kept an eye on the boy. The man had walked to the top floor early in the morning, watching the family as they left. But the boy hadn't been with the parents when they left the room. For a long time, the man thought they had left the boy inside the room, but then much to his luck, the boy had come storming up the stairs looking tired and red-eyed. He had knocked on the door frantically until a cabin-boy had unlocked the door for him.

Now he was leaving the room again. The man couldn't believe his luck. He followed him closely with his eyes. The boy walked through the hallway towards the stairs. The man followed him a few steps behind. He knew who the boy was. He knew who his father was very well. That the father was a world-famous racecar-driver only made it so much more fun. Spectacular even.

The man followed Alberto Colombo into the casino, where he was almost alone. He watched him throw a credit card on the counter of the bar.

"Your most expensive whiskey, please."

"That'll be the Macallan from 1926," the bartender said, while serving Alberto the glass. "It's three thousand Euros per glass. Enjoy."

The man sat next to him on a stool and ordered a coffee.

Alberto Colombo was looking at his whiskey.

"Aren't you going to drink that?" the man asked without looking at the boy. "Quite an expensive drink to simply let it evaporate."

Alberto scoffed. "I don't even like whiskey."

The man drank from his coffee. "Then why did you order it?"

"I don't know. To get back at my parents, I guess. You know, to be spiteful," Alberto answered with a sigh. "Guess I'm just mad at them. They never care about anything but their money and their things. I don't count. I'm not important."

The man finished his cup. "I know a thing or two about being spiteful," he said. "Maybe there's a better way. Something a little more fun."

Alberto looked at him and smiled. "You mean like drugs? You know how to get any?"

The man still didn't look directly at him. He kept staring into the mirror behind the bar where he could study the boy's every move without him noticing it. He liked what he saw. He especially liked the boy's silky smooth olive skin. He shrugged and drank his coffee again.

"Maybe I do. Maybe I don't."

"I have money," Alberto said.

"I noticed."

"So, can you do it? Can you get me something?"

"You really want it, huh?"

"I do. I do. I just want to have fun and forget. I never get to do anything fun. After this trip, I'm going back to my boarding school in France. It's so boring there you wouldn't believe it. I need to have some fun, please. I'll pay you three times the price you usually demand."

The man finally turned his head and looked directly at Alberto.

Fishy, fishy in the brook. Papa caught him on a hook. Mama fried him up at home. Now don't choke on a bone!

"You will now, will you? Well, I think we just might be able to come to an agreement then." The man threw a bill on the counter and emptied his cup. He didn't look at the boy when he spoke to him.

"Meet me downstairs on the lower deck in ten minutes. Come alone. Bring the money."

9

APRIL 1976

The twins didn't know where they were when they opened their eyes. It was dark. They both had a severe headache.

"Where are we?"

"I don't know."

A door soon opened and a flock of men entered. The light was turned on. It was bright and hurt the twin's eyes at first, until they got used to it. The men stared at the boys. They were talking amongst each other while scrutinizing the boys, studying them. A voice resounded in the windowless room. It belonged to a small man with a sweaty face and stubble.

"Gentlemen. I give you the *Spider-boys!*" he yelled.

There was talking amongst the spectators. The voice continued.

"Two heads, three legs and four hands."

"Is it one person or two?" someone asked.

"Yeah, do we have to pay double?" another one yelled.

Then they laughed. A cold sinister laughter that made Tweedledee and Tweedledum shiver in fear. Someone in the crowd raised his hand.

"One million Lire."

"Two," another said.

"Two and a half," a third man said.

"Three," the first said again.

The twins looked, frightened, from one face to another. They were slowly realizing what was going on. They were being sold to the highest bidder.

They looked at each other and started talking between themselves in their own made-up language.

"I'm scared."

"So am I."

Suddenly, another voice resounded from back in the crowd. It cut its way through the cold air. Everybody went quiet.

"Ten million Lire!"

Everyone turned to look. Even the twins stopped talking and looked at who had given this big offer. It was the only woman in the room. She was tall and wide at the shoulders. Her face wore thick layers of make-up to cover up her age. She walked forward with a big smile on her face. Her black hair was covered by a colorful scarf.

"I'll pay ten million Lire for them," she repeated.

"Sold!" the small man said and shook her hand.

The woman looked at the twins. They whimpered in fright. "Good. Bring it to my truck outside."

The twins could hardly manage to protest before a black plastic bag was put over their heads and they felt themselves get lifted up. They were thrown inside the truck and soon it started moving. The twins held each other's hands as they drove.

They sensed the truck come to a halt, then the door was opened and hands were on them once again. They were carried somewhere and thrown on the hard ground. Then everything went quiet. They didn't dare to speak for a long time.

"I don't think anyone is here," Tweedledum said.

"I'm scared," Tweedledee said.

"I'm gonna take off the plastic bag now," Tweedledum said.

"Don't. Maybe they'll be angry and hurt us."

"I want this thing off."

He pulled the plastic bag off, then gasped.

"What?" Tweedledee said.

"Take your bag off as well. It's safe. We're alone."

Tweedledee grabbed his bag as well and pulled it off. "Where are we?" he asked with terror in his voice.

"I don't know. It looks like they put us in a cage."

10

APRIL 2014

I was exhausted once we got back to the ship. The entire day we had been traveling by bus, walking up the volcano and walking through the old city of Pompeii. It was every bit as splendid as I remembered it, but a lot for just one day. Especially with my mom and dad, who had been acting like teenagers all day. They were constantly flirting, kissing and sitting on each other's laps. They were giggling and not paying any attention to what the tour guide told us.

I thought Victor would be the one to drive me nuts, but he acted really nice and remained calm during most of the trip. He never threw a fit or screamed because someone touched him. I had feared going out with this many people in public since it was always hard on him, but he had managed it very well and I decided to let him get some ice cream in the room once we got back. We had eaten in a small restaurant close to Pompeii, but there hadn't been time for dessert before we had to get back on the bus.

We walked towards the entrance of the ship, my mom and dad falling behind as usual, when Victor suddenly grabbed my hand. I gasped and looked down at him. He didn't look at me. I drew in a deep breath and enjoyed feeling him close to me. I squeezed his hand gently and closed my eyes for just a second to take in the rare moment. Christoffer kept walking and didn't seem to notice.

"What a great day, huh buddy?" I asked.

Suddenly, he looked at me. He lifted his face and I saw his eyes behind the brown curls.

"Someone is going to die," he said.

"What? What are you saying? Why would you say something like that? Don't say stuff like that, Victor. It scares me."

Victor let go of my hand. My parents caught up with us. "What's going on?" my mom asked cheerfully.

I shook my head and continued to walk. "Nothing. Victor is just acting and talking weird."

"Ah, don't worry. He's a boy. They say strange stuff just to get a reaction from you. It's perfectly normal. He's just playing around."

"Maybe."

"You know you're not doing him any favors by treating him like a baby," my mom said.

"What's that supposed to mean?" I asked.

"You know what I mean," my mom said.

I looked at Victor while we walked. He didn't care that he had upset me. That was part of his condition. He didn't understand what would upset others. I had no idea how to teach him not to say and do stuff that made others feel uncomfortable. They had told me in school they couldn't have him there if he did anything to upset the other students again...like the time when he showed them a PowerPoint presentation of how to decapitate a human head when he was telling about the French Revolution. I talked to him about it over and over again, but it was no use. He simply didn't understand.

We walked up the ramp towards the ship's entrance and walked inside. On the penthouse floor, there was turmoil of some sort. A woman and a man were standing in the corridor, talking to some of the ship's personnel. They seemed upset. I walked with Victor and Christoffer towards our door while listening in on their conversation.

"How could he just disappear? I don't understand this," the woman said. "I told him to stay in the room till we came back. When we got here, the room was empty. His phone is still in there. Where is he?"

"I don't know Signora Colombo," the man in uniform said. "But we'll make sure to look for him. The ship doesn't leave until tomorrow afternoon. I'm sure he'll turn up. Maybe he's somewhere on the ship. Maybe he went onshore for a little while. He's fourteen, you say? Well, at that age, they tend to do stuff on their own, right? Let's calm down and wait. He'll probably show up tonight. It's very easy to get lost here on our ship."

Colombo? As in the racecar driver Alonzo Colombo?

I looked at the couple and recognized the man's face. He looked angry.

"I can't believe this. I'm gonna...that boy is...It's all your fault," he said to his wife. "You smother him. I tell you not to. He needs discipline." Alonzo Colombo now looked at the man in uniform. "I tell you, if he doesn't show up tonight, I'll sue your company."

"Surely, Signor Colombo it is not our fault..."

"Well, it's not my fault, is it? It has to be someone's, right? I'm betting it's yours. I'll sue you for everything you've got."

"Let's not get ourselves agitated here," the uniformed man said. "I'll have all my staff looking for him and I'm sure he'll show up."

APRIL 2014

Alberto opened his eyes with a gasp. The man's face was close to his. He was smiling eerily.

"Well, hello there."

"What happened?" Alberto asked.

The man tilted his head, then giggled for his answer.

Alberto sat up. His head was hurting. He was dizzy. "Where am I?"

"Welcome to my humble chambers," the man said and bowed in his long black coat.

"What is this place?"

"We're on the lower deck. Take a good look at it. It'll be the last place you see." The man spun and made his black coat twirl theatrically in the air.

"Excuse me?" Alberto asked.

"Yeeezz?"

"I just...It sounded like you said..."

"Well I did," the man exclaimed. "I indeed did."

Alberto looked at him. Suddenly, he seemed really creepy. Alberto hadn't noticed earlier but the man's body seemed funny. Alberto watched as he walked to his suitcase and opened it. He started taking out what looked like bottles of chemicals with warning labels on them, then some strange instruments and tools. Alberto felt an eerie sensation in his body.

What the hell is this?

"So, just give me my drugs and I'll be out of here," he said. He could hear how his voice was shivering as he spoke.

The man stopped what he was doing and turned his head like an owl to look at Alberto. Then he laughed.

"What's so funny?" Alberto asked.

The man pulled out a scalpel and showed it to Alberto.

"What're you going to do with that?" he asked with a trembling voice.

The man giggled. "I need something from you."

He came closer and Alberto pulled his legs up under his knees and pulled backwards till his back hit the wall. The man sat on the edge of the bed. He was still smiling. He stroked Alberto's cheek.

"So pretty. So beautiful."

Alberto pushed the man's hand away. The man grabbed his hand and held it tightly.

"You're hurting me," Alberto whimpered.

The man studied Alberto's arm and ran a finger across his skin. "Such beautiful skin," he mumbled. "Even prettier when you get closer to it. We'll have to make sure nothing happens to it, won't we? So precious. So soft."

Alberto tried to pull his arm back, but couldn't. The man had extremely strong hands. He was stronger than he looked. Alberto was terrified. He didn't like the way the man looked at him.

Mom? Dad? Please help me. Please come for me? I'll never do anything bad again. I promise. It doesn't matter that you don't notice me. I'll never ask you for anything again. Please, dear God. Help me.

The man looked like he enjoyed watching Alberto in distress. He stroked Alberto's cheek again. "There's someone I want you to meet," he said.

"Who...? Who...Is that?"

The man giggled, then took off his coat.

The sight that met Alberto was made by such a horror he wasn't even able to scream. Nor did he feel anything when the scalpel quickly penetrated the skin and slit his throat.

12

APRIL 1976

They came in the next morning. The twins were sleeping when they entered the room. The broad woman was flanked by two men. They were yelling when they opened the cage and took out the twins by pulling their arms. The twins screamed in fear as they were dragged out on the floor.

The men stripped them down before they started beating them, taking turns throwing punches at their faces. The twins screamed in pain and anguish. The woman stepped forward, pulled a knife, and started cutting their faces, arms and legs. One of the men punched them in the belly. Then he pulled a knife with the intention of stabbing them. The twins screamed.

"Not there," the woman said. "Only in places that are visible. We want to increase sympathy not disable them further."

The beating and disfiguring continued for an hour before they finally stopped. Then the twins were dressed in new clothes, mostly rags, and were carried out to the truck and thrown inside. A few moments later, they were pulled out. Blood was still dripping from the cuts in their faces. They were dragged into an open space and put next to a building. The woman put a tin cup and a sign in front of them stating:

We are the Spider-boys. We're hungry. Please help.

The woman patted them on the head. "There. You're ready. Make mama some money. Remember, pity pays."

Then she left. Soon, people walking past started noticing the boys and, not long after, a crowd had gathered in front of them. Tourists were taking pictures, others were chatting amongst themselves and pointing their fingers at the twins. Some were even laughing, but most felt sorry for them and eventually threw bills in their cup. The twins were so badly beaten, they could hardly see out of their eyes and, if they did, all they saw were disgusted frowning faces and occasional merciful looks. Meanwhile, in between the many people in the crowd, the woman's helpers, mostly younger children, crept up from behind and put their small fingers in the staring tourists' pockets, pulling out their wallets along with anything else of value.

Surprised by this, the twins tried to speak, but nothing but groaning and growling sounds exited their badly beaten mouths. They tried to get up and crawl away, but the pain in their arms made them fall down again. The crowd gasped. The twins tried again, then staggered back and forth on their hands. The crowd suddenly clapped and cheered and started throwing money at them.

That was when some of them realized something was wrong.

"Hey. Who stole my wallet?" one man yelled.

Everybody in the crowd reached in their pockets and purses.

"Mine is gone too."

"And mine!"

The crowd soon turned and looked at the twins. The pity in their eyes was gone, replaced by anger.

"Get them," someone yelled.

Realizing the danger, the twins crawled sideways like a crab as fast as they could, but it wasn't fast enough. The crowd grabbed them and started beating them. Meanwhile, the children and the woman disappeared. Men in the crowd kicked the twins and yelled at them to give their money back and it wasn't until the police arrived that they stopped. One of the officers who had picked them up and taken them to the station continued to hit them with his truncheon while yelling at them.

He stopped when his superior entered the room. "What do we have here?" the superior asked.

"They're part of the Slovenski Gang, sir."

"The gypsies?"

"Yes, sir. They were stealing people's wallets downtown. I'm trying to get them to tell us where they're hiding."

The twins were crying and whimpering in pain, hardly able to breathe, let alone speak and defend themselves. They wanted badly to tell their story, but had only enough strength to whisper.

"My God they're creepy," the superior said. "Disgusting creatures. What are they? One or two?"

"I don't know, sir."

"It doesn't matter. Have them speak and then get them out of here. I get sick just by looking at them."

"Yes, sir."

13

APRIL 2014

B ack in my suite, I ordered some ice cream for the boys and me. We ate it while watching the History channel where they showed an old World War II documentary. Victor loved this kind of stuff and I relaxed by checking my Facebook and playing Candy Crush on my iPad. Christoffer went to his room to read, once he had finished his ice cream.

My editor had written an e-mail telling me my latest manuscript *Peek-A-Boo, I see You* that I had just finished before we left was amazing and she was already talking to a German publisher who was interested in buying the rights to it.

I didn't feel good about the book. It was good. It was well written and it was a great story. I knew that. But I had debated for a long time whether to write it or not. Mostly because it was exactly what my former mailman Arne Holm wanted me to do. To write his story. He had told me that was the entire idea for him to do all those awful things to me and my family and to kill those people, it was to have me write about it, to have me write his story. So, at first, I had refused to do so. I didn't want him to have the plea-sure of succeeding. But the more I thought about it, the more I realized it was an important story to tell. Especially now that the current Danish government was cutting off the funding to a lot of institutions like Hummelgaarden and placing children with mental disabilities in normal classrooms where they didn't get the help they needed. Just like Victor. So I wrote the book for my own sake, I kept telling myself. It was for Victor. I was hoping it would stir up some debate and maybe make people aware of the problems. But it bothered me that somewhere in a Danish prison sat Arne Holm with a smile on his face. As soon as the book was published, he would think he had succeeded. And I didn't want him to think that. I wanted him to think he failed. But how could I? So I had written a fore-word to the book where I explained my own and Victor's situation and the reason for writing the book.

But who was I kidding? Arne Holm had planned this all the way and he knew I would eventually write his story. I just had to come to terms with that.

I dozed off on the couch while Victor indulged himself in the horrors of the World War. It had been a great day for him. He truly enjoyed walking the streets of Pompeii, knowing it had all once been covered in ashes and people had died in their houses and in the street. It fascinated him.

I woke up to the sound of my phone. It was Morten calling.

"Hey. Just wanted to reach you before you go to bed. How's the cruise-life treating you?"

"Excellent. Went on a great trip today. I just posted some pictures on Facebook if you want to see them."

"How's Victor?"

I smiled. I loved how he always worried about my kids. It suddenly struck me that I hardly knew his daughter. But it was harder with her since she was very jealous and didn't really want to get to know me.

"He's fine. He had a blast at Pompeii today. Christoffer too, even if he didn't find the dead people as fascinating as Victor. He loved the volcano, though."

"That's good."

"How are things back home on the island?" I asked.

"Nice and quiet. Just the way I like it. I'm on night duty, so I'm about to take off now. How are the lovebirds?"

I groaned. "They're fine too. A little annoying if you ask me, but hey, it's better than them hating each other, right?"

Morten laughed. "Sure is. Well take care of everyone and I'll talk to you tomorrow, alright?"

"Have a good shift."

"Thanks."

I hung up, still smiling. I really loved Morten. He was so easy, so uncomplicated. A new show started on the History channel.

"It's time to get ready for bed, buddy," I said and looked at the clock. It was important for Victor that some things like his bedtime remained the way it always was. Especially when we were out. Ole Knudsen had taught me that. Victor needed clear limits and boundaries.

"I want to see the next show," he said. "It's about the children born after the Vietnam War. They have all kinds of deformities. Lots of Vietnamese children are suffering from devastating effects of toxic herbicide sprayed by US Army forty years ago."

I looked at the screen where a woman was holding her strangely deformed child into the air. Then there was a teenager who was bed-ridden because his feet were bent backwards and he couldn't walk. He was also deaf, the speaker told us.

"That's just a freak-show," I said and grabbed the remote.

Victor took it out of my hand.

"Victor!" I said. It was so unlike him to do anything like this. "Give it back."

Victor didn't look at me. He stared at the floor while speaking. "I want to see this."

"Well, you can't. It's time for bed now. You've had enough death and destruction today."

Clear limits, Emma. You're doing the right thing.

"It's important. I want to SEE it!"

"Victor. Don't you raise your voice at me. I'm your mother and I decide what you watch. And it is time for bed now. No more TV. If you don't give me the remote, there will be no TV tomorrow either."

Victor held onto the remote. He stared at the screen. A little girl lacked an arm and a leg.

"Victor, this is disgusting. Why do you want to watch this anyway?"

"Am I disgusting too?" he asked, while his eyes were fixated on the screen.

My heart dropped. Was that how he saw himself?

"No! Don't you ever think that about yourself."

"But I'm just like them, Mom. I'm a freak too."

I almost burst into tears, but managed to hold them back. I grabbed the remote from his hand and finally turned off the TV. "You are not a freak, Victor. Listen to me. You're not a freak."

"But what's the difference between them and me?"

I exhaled deeply. "Well most of them can't walk or take care of themselves. You can. You can do everything by yourself and you're smart, Victor. You're smarter than most people."

Victor shook his head. It was the first time I had seen him like this, questioning himself and who he was.

"No. I'm like them. I'm a circus-freak. That's what they call me at school."

I closed my eyes for a short second and took a deep breath. I knew this would come eventually. I knew they would start picking on him in school. It was bound to happen. I had just hoped he wouldn't care.

"I'm sorry that they do that, Victor. I'll have to talk to your teacher about it. Kids can be really cruel sometimes. Especially when someone is a little different."

Victor sat on the bed with his head bowed. He nodded. He was drumming his fingers on his lap. "I am different. I know I am. Why am I different Mommy?"

"I don't know, Victor. You have what they call a light autism. It makes you really smart and special, but also different in the way you act around people. That can be hard for other kids to accept."

Victor went quiet all of a sudden. He stopped drumming on his pants.

"What's wrong buddy?" I asked.

"Call a doctor," he said.

"What? Why? Is something wrong with you? Are you alright?"

Victor turned his head and looked at me. Then he screamed: "CALL A DOCTOR!"

14

APRIL 2014

S tartled, I jumped up and ran to the phone. I called the front desk downstairs.

"Yes?" the lady asked.

"I need a doctor to the penthouse suites," I said. I looked at Victor who was walking in circles, massaging his temples while humming. I was scared he was having a seizure, but he wasn't shaking or rolling his eyes like he usually did.

"What is the emergency, Mrs.?"

"Mrs. Frost. I have to say I'm not sure. But my son is not feeling well, I think." I bit my lip, knowing it sounded like I was just a crazy overprotective mother.

"Okay," the woman said. "We have a doctor onboard. I'll send him to your room right away."

"Thanks." I hung up, slightly surprised that the woman had taken me this seriously. I looked at Victor.

The door to Christoffer's room opened and he peeked out. "What's going on? Is Victor alright?"

"Yes. Everything is fine, Christoffer. Just go to bed. Victor is just having a fit that's all."

"Do you need any help, Emma?" he asked.

I was moved by his compassion. I wasn't used to that from a boy his age. "No. It's sweet of you. But I'll take care of it."

"Okay," Christoffer said, and closed the door again.

I stared at Victor. His body was shaking all over. "Could you please tell me what is going on? Why did I have to call for a doctor?" I asked.

Victor was humming and walking. It was about to drive me nuts. "Please, just talk to me, buddy. Tell me what's going on."

"Three, four, five...three, four, five," he kept repeating.

"Three, four, five? What does that mean?" I asked.

But Victor had somehow escaped to his own little world and I could no longer reach him. He was humming and saying the numbers over and over again.

There was a knock on the door and I ran to open it. Outside stood a small elderly man in a white shirt with a brown bag in his hand.

"Did someone call for a doctor?"

"Yes. Yes, I did," I said. Then I looked up at the door leading to my suite and saw the number three hundred and thirty eight. I looked at the doctor.

"Three, four, five," I said.

He looked at me like I had lost my mind.

"Three, four, five," I repeated.

"Excuse me? I was told there was some sort of emergency?" the doctor asked.

"Yes. I believe it is in room three hundred and forty-five," I said and closed the door behind me, making sure it locked. "Follow me."

We walked down the corridor and I knocked on the door leading to room three hundred and forty five. "Hello?"

No one answered.

"Listen. I...," the doctor said. I could tell he thought I had lost it.

"Wait a second," I said and knocked again. "Hello?"

There still was no answer. I had a bad feeling. "I think we need to get in there immediately," I said. "I bet you have a key?"

"There is nothing here that indicates that it should be necessary. I really don't think..."

"But I do. There is something very wrong here," I said. "We need to go in immediately."

The doctor inhaled deeply and looked at me. "Are you sure, I really don't want to..."

"Just do it, damn it!"

The doctor shook his head and found the key-card in his pocket. He slid it through the reader and the door clicked open. I stormed in, thinking I was either going to save someone's life or get arrested for breaking and entering.

Luckily it was the first of the two. On the floor inside the suite, I spotted Mrs. Colombo lying pale and lifeless. The doctor gasped and stormed towards her.

"She's out cold," he said and kneeled next to her. He turned her to the side to prevent choking.

I spotted something on the table and picked it up. "Insulin. She must be a diabetic," I said.

"Let me see," the doctor said. "She's probably suffering from hypoglycemia. I have injectable glucagon in my bag." He opened his bag, pulled something out and gave the woman a shot in the thigh. Soon after, she woke up. The doctor helped her get to her bed.

"What happened?" she asked confused.

"You fainted," the doctor said and put a pillow behind her neck.

"Alberto," the woman suddenly cried. "Is he back?"

"You need to get some rest," the doctor said. "Where is Mr. Colombo?"

"He went downstairs to look for our son. He's been missing since last night. We thought he just went to the casino. We know he spent some money there last night, but he never came back. I guess I got a little upset and forgot to eat."

"I'm sure your son is fine," the doctor said. "You shouldn't let yourself get upset like this. Now let us get ahold of your husband and get him to come back here."

"I can call him," Mrs. Colombo said. "If you'll just hand me my phone over there."

15

APRIL 2014

Mr. Colombo was clearly distressed when he stormed through the door to his own suite. His wife was still lying in her bed.

"Ivana," he yelled. "Are you alright?"

Ivana explained to her husband what had happened. He grabbed my hand and shook it. I felt slightly star-struck. Alonzo Colombo was probably the biggest star in race driving in Europe right now. Not that I knew much about the sport, but I did know that he drove for Ferrari and that he was a seven-time Formula One World Champion. He was regarded as one of the greatest drivers of all time.

"Thank you for being there," he said.

I smiled and blushed. "No problem, Mr. Colombo. I'm just glad I could help."

"Call me Alonzo, please. Let me know if there is anything we can do for you in return."

I shook my head. "I don't need anything, thank you."

Alonzo Colombo turned to look at his wife. "I told her all day to eat. But she's been so upset over Alberto's disappearance that she could hardly get anything down. I had a feeling something like this might happen. I never should have left you."

"Did you find him?" Ivana asked nervously.

Alonzo bit his lip and shook his head. "No. I talked to a guy working at the casino who dealt black-jack cards for him early in the morning. One of the cabin-boys told me he helped Alberto get into the suite around eight in the morning. Alberto told him he had lost his key. The bartender at the casino served him a drink around eight-thirty. After that, the leads end. No one has seen him since then."

"So he was fine this morning? That's a relief," Ivana said.

"Yes. It is. But what worries me is that no one has seen him since. And I've been all over the place. The upper deck, the pool area, the wave pool, all the bars and restaurants in this place. Even the tennis courts. He was nowhere." Alonzo Colombo sighed. "I don't understand where he can be. I mean, he was drinking in the morning hours...maybe he's passed out somewhere?"

"Could he have left the ship?" I asked. They both looked at me. "Not that it's any of my business."

"Oh my God, Alonzo. The woman is right. What if he came back here, saw my note and knew we were angry, then left the ship?" Ivana had tears in her big eyes. "Oh my God, Alonzo. What if he has run away?"

"Now don't get yourself upset again, Mrs. Colombo," the doctor said. "You need to get something to eat right away. Let me order some food for you."

Ivana didn't answer the doctor. She kept looking at her husband. Alonzo Colombo was getting red cheeks. "He knows he's not allowed to leave the ship on his own," he hissed angrily.

"Oh God, Alonzo. It's all our fault. We've been too harsh on the boy and now he has run away."

Alonzo's anger turned to sadness. "It's me isn't it? I've been too selfish. I know I have. It's been all about me the last several years."

"You think he ran away?" Ivana asked.

"Let's not jump to conclusions," Alonzo said. "He could still be on the ship passed out somewhere, drunk." Alonzo hit his fist into the dresser next to him. "I can't believe they would give alcohol to a fourteen year-old. I'm gonna sue those bastards."

"You really think your anger will help get our boy back home?" Ivana asked.

I looked at the doctor, who was still on the phone ordering food for Ivana Colombo. Meanwhile, the couple was fighting heavily now and yelling at each other. I was starting to get really uncomfortable.

"Why would he be drinking in the first place? He's just a kid," Alonzo said. "It's all your fault. You should have kept an eye on him."

"Typically of you to push the responsibility over on me. Aren't you the father?"

"You tell me. You'd been with so many guys when I met you, he could be anyone's, couldn't he?"

"How dare you?"

This was getting to a point where I was no longer comfortable in the room.

The doctor hung up. "There. Food is on its way up. Shouldn't be long. Now, remember to eat. I don't want to have to come up here again."

Ivana wasn't listening to him. She was snorting and staring angrily at her husband. Alonzo grabbed a vase and threw it against the wall in anger. It shattered all over the floor.

"Maybe it's time to call the police?" I said. "The ship leaves tonight and, if you want to find your son before that, you might need some help. Especially if he's gone into town."

They both looked at me like I had overstepped some boundary and entered where I didn't belong. I shrugged. "Just a suggestion. I don't know if they'll do much when he hasn't been gone for longer than he has, but it's worth a shot. After all, with your name and status, they might be willing to bend the rules a little. What if it was a kidnapping? It wouldn't look good on the city's reputation would it? Sorrento is known as a place many celebrities and rich people spend their vacations. They'd want to have a reputation for being a safe place wouldn't they? Anyway, it was just a suggestion. I need to get back. I left two children all alone in my suite. Hope you feel better soon Mrs. Colombo."

16

APRIL 1978

He had kept the twins. No one else wanted anything to do with them, so no one questioned it when Officer Maraldi decided to take them back to his own house and lock them inside his basement. At first, he had no idea what to do with them. He kept them locked away and fed them using a bowl he placed on the floor like they were animals. They didn't speak at all. They never told him where to find the rest of the Slovenski Gang and it irritated him that he had come so close to nailing the gang, but still hadn't succeeded. The gang still roamed the streets of his district in the city of Rome and there were days when he was certain they were laughing at him while they did. Every day, he had tourists come to his station and report stolen passports, wallets and cameras. And every day he had to tell them the same thing.

"We'll look for your stolen goods, but I'm afraid I can't promise you much."

It annoyed him immensely and, at first, he thought that if he brought the twins to his house, he would be able to get them to talk eventually and they would tell him about the gang's whereabouts, but it never happened. He tried everything. He beat the crap out of them, he fed them and promised ice cream for dessert if they told him, then beat them again because they didn't answer. He tried it all, but they had shut up and refused to speak a word.

Officer Maraldi knew they were capable of talking. He heard them at night speaking to one another. Lying in his bed upstairs, he could hear their puny voices through the ventilation shaft. But he didn't understand a word they spoke.

Two years had passed now since he brought them to his house and he had found a new way they could be of use to him. It was actually his colleague, Luigi who had come up with the idea. He was the only one who knew that the twins were in Maraldi's house.

"We could make money off of them," he said one night when they were hanging out in a park nearby playing Bocce.

"How so?" Officer Maraldi asked, then threw his metal ball. It landed in the sand with a thud.

"Fights," Luigi said and walked to the end of the lane, lifted his ball, aimed and threw it. It landed closer than Maraldi's. Luigi smiled. "We can arrange fights with them."

Maraldi liked the idea right away. So one Friday late afternoon, he walked down into the basement. Afraid of getting beaten up again, the twins crawled backwards into a corner as soon as they saw him. Maraldi covered them up in a blanket and tied them down, then carried them into his old truck and drove them downtown. Luigi met him behind the old building at the harbor. Maraldi opened the truck and they carried the twins out.

They didn't remove the blanket from their faces until they were inside the ring. Then Maraldi and Luigi both walked behind the closed gate. The twins both looked at Maraldi. For a split second, he wondered if this was going to be the last he saw of them. There was no way they would survive this, he thought to himself.

When the pit-bull entered the arena, the twins turned to look at it. Then they whimpered loudly. The crowd laughed and then clapped. Bets were made and people were watching the spectacle with great enthusiasm and fascination. Never had they seen anything like this.

"Quite the crowd those *Spider-boys* of yours can draw," the guy arranging the fight said to Maraldi. "It's the biggest crowd this year. Too bad we can only do this once." Then he left laughing.

The pit-bull growled. It came closer to the twins. It was drooling and snarling. The twins crab-walked backwards. The crowd cheered on the dog. The twins looked up at Maraldi like they expected him to step in.

But, of course, he didn't. He watched the spectacle with as much joy and captivation as the rest of the crowd. The dog roared, then jumped them and let its teeth sink into their back. Blood gushed out from the wound and the twins both screamed. The dog drew back, then circled them before it attacked again, biting one of their arms, forcing them to fall to the ground. The crowd was cheering...yelling and screaming for the dog to kill them.

Kill. Kill. Kill.

Maraldi felt a chill of joy. This was truly enjoyable. More than he had ever expected it to be.

But, as it turned out, Maraldi and the cheering crowd had completely underestimated the twins' strength. Just as they had both of their faces in the dust and were bleeding from their many wounds, they did something officer Maraldi had never seen them do before. Something he wasn't even aware that they were capable of. Somehow, they managed to rise to their three legs and stood tall in front of the dog. They clenched their four fists and started hitting the dog non-stop. They swung their arms like cartwheels and knocked the dog back with such strength, the crowd went completely quiet.

A few seconds later, they burst into another cheer. This time for the twins.

Spider-boys, spider-boys!

Maraldi watched with a strange enthrallment as the twins threw themselves at the dog and, with their bare hands, grabbed its neck and strangled it till it fell to the ground. People held their breath while waiting for the dog to get back up. But it didn't move. It lay on the dirty floor completely lifeless.

The twins crumbled back down and started walking on their hands again, crawling like a spider while the crowd cheered and clapped.

Maraldi was clapping wildly too. He couldn't stop smiling and was hearing nothing but that clinking, clanking sound of money inside of his mind.

A buck or a pound is all that makes the world go 'round.

17

APRIL 2014

The man was tired, but he hardly noticed it anymore. He had been working all night on his project, cutting and sewing...Bits and pieces, making it all fit together nicely.

The boy's skin turned out to be even nicer than he had dared to hope for...Soft and smooth, very elastic. Perfect for his purpose.

The man smiled as he carefully held parts of it up in the light and turned it. He sat down with a piece of the boy's skin and looked at it for a moment, as if it was a present he needed to enjoy. Then he sewed it onto another piece.

He was working hard, but enjoying every single moment of it. On the table next to him lay the remains of a skinned body...something that, to most people, would represent horror and their worst nightmare, but to the man it was pure beauty.

The man yawned, but it was not time to sleep yet. First, he had to finish his project. Even if it was the middle of the night, the man felt energized as he looked at his finished product. He stood up and held it out for a better look, smiling from ear to ear at his accomplishments. A few spots of blood were removed with some rubbing alcohol. The finished jacket was put on the bed and the remains of the boy thrown inside the bathtub in the bathroom. Wearing thick gloves, he poured acid on the remains of the boy, covering the entire body in it. Slowly, the bones and the meat started smoking and melting and soon there was nothing left. The man then opened the plug and let it all wash out, knowing it was going to end up in the ocean.

"There, Deedee. All traces are gone. No one will ever know."

"Are you done with my present?"

The man put the acid and the gloves back in his suitcase with the rest of his equipment. Then, he smiled from ear to ear. "Yes. Yes, I am, Deedee. It's all finished. I'm certain you will be pleased."

"Can I see it? Can I see it?"

The man went into the bedroom of his lower deck suite. There was a case on the bed. He was struggling slightly with the pain in his shoulder, but decided to ignore it. He had, after all, just cleaned the wounds. Of course it was going to hurt a little. It didn't matter.

The man sat on the edge of the bed. He put a hand on the case and opened the lid.

"I hate being in this thing," Deedee said.

"I know," the man answered. "But take a look at this."

He held the jacket up in the air for Deedee to see.

"It's beautiful," Deedee said with a gasp.

"I know. It's perfect for you. Let me help you put it on."

The man carefully placed the jacket on Deedee, making sure it fit nicely. "It's a little too big, but I can adjust that if you like," he said.

"No. It's perfect," Deedee said. "How do I look?"

The man couldn't stop smiling. "You look great, Deedee. You look really great."

He grabbed his camera and took a picture.

"Don't," Deedee said. "I don't like looking at myself. You know that."

"But I really want to take your picture. You look so good. Don't be shy."

"Okay then. If you must."

The man smiled and took a series of pictures. He showed one of them to Deedee.

"How handsome I look," Deedee said.

"Yes."

"Thank you."

"We're not done yet," the man said. "There is still a lot of work to do. This is just the beginning, Deedee. Soon, I'll have all of you dressed and then we go for the most important thing. Do you know what that is, Deedee?"

"My face."

"Yes. We need to get you a new face. And I know exactly who is going to give you that."

18

APRIL 2014

None of us slept well that night. Except for Christoffer who slept like a baby and never even noticed that Victor kept having nightmares and woke up screaming in the darkness. I did what I could to calm him down. When I asked him the next morning what he dreamt, he simply said...

"That I didn't have a face."

We took off on our trip to the Isle of Capri. We saw the Blue Grotto and all the other sights the island had to offer...like the small famous harbor Marina Piccola, the Belvedere of Tragara—a high panoramic promenade lined with villa, the Faraglioni—the limestone crags called sea stacks that project above the sea, the town of Anacapri, and the ruins of the Imperial Roman villas. I found everything very interesting, especially since I had never been there before. But Victor didn't find any of it as alluring as Pompeii. He was very quiet most of the day and I wondered if something was bothering him...If it was those dreams that wouldn't leave him. Christoffer, on the other hand, seemed to enjoy this trip more than the one on the previous day. He thought the Blue Grotto was spectacular and wouldn't stop talking about it afterwards.

We came back to the ship late in the afternoon. I was exhausted from all the walking and threw myself on the couch and took off my shoes as soon as we landed. I had paid for a nice big lunch at a wonderful small Italian place on the island, so none of us were hungry and we decided to meet up and eat a late dinner on the boat.

"We could use a nap," my mom said when we said goodbye in the hallway. She poked my dad in the side with her elbow and winked. "Right, papa bear?"

Papa bear?

"That sounds nice," my dad chuckled. "Mama bear."

Oh my God!

Now I was just lying on the couch while Victor indulged himself in Christoffer's book. Christoffer watched TV. I closed my eyes and dozed off. I was awakened by a message on the speakers from our captain.

"Due to unforeseen circumstances, we have to postpone the departure from Sorrento till later tonight. We hope to be able to set off towards Sicily before midnight. Thank you for your understanding."

I looked at the boys. Victor didn't seem to care, but Christoffer looked at me for an answer.

"Postpone the departure?" I asked and sat up.

"Why?" Christoffer asked.

I shrugged. "I have no idea. Maybe it's something technical."

Or could it have something to do with Mr. and Mrs. Colombo? Hadn't they found the boy?

I heard voices in the hallway and got up. "Stay here," I said to the boys and left the suite.

As if Victor would ever leave the suite. If it was up to him, he'd stay in there the entire trip.

In the hallway, a crowd had gathered, surrounding a man in uniform. Voices were debating vividly. I walked further down and realized there was turmoil near the end of the hallway, down by Alonzo Colombo's suite. I walked faster and suddenly spotted a flock of police officers standing outside his suite. Some walked inside, while others worked outside. Some were wearing blue plastic suits. I'd been around long enough to know a forensic team when I saw one.

So they finally called the police for help. Good for them. It seemed like they were doing a very thorough job. A guy was dusting for fingerprints on the door. As I was about to turn around and go back, I saw Alonzo Colombo coming out of the suite. I smiled until I noticed he wasn't walking willingly. He was flanked by two officers and had his hands cuffed behind his back. I gasped.

What the heck was going on here?

Alonzo Colombo was taken away and he didn't even look at me as they walked past me.

"I heard he killed his wife." The voice behind me belonged to my dad. I turned and looked into his eyes.

"He did what?"

"The couple staying in the suite next to us told us he killed her this morning. They were fighting loudly and then he pulled a gun on her. Shot her right through the temple." My dad pointed at his own head to show me. I was appalled.

"They say he probably killed his son as well. He's been missing since yesterday morning, as far as I was told. Mr. Colombo probably threw him overboard or something."

"Wow. I...don't know what to say. I was with them last night because the wife was sick...I...They were fighting and he seemed to have a temper and everything, but this...I never suspected he would...I mean, it was his son?"

My dad shrugged. "Guess the tabloids will have a lot to talk about the coming days, huh?"

"I can't believe it. He seemed so upset that the son was missing."

"He's probably just a great actor. They say he tried to tell the police that the wife committed suicide. He even placed the gun in her hand and everything. He probably thought everyone else had left the deck to go on trips, so no one would hear anything, since we're so far away from everyone else on this cruise, but the Swedish couple next to our suite were home. The wife didn't feel well and they decided to stay onboard. They called the police when they heard the shot. Personnel from the ship were all over him before he could escape."

"But they never found the boy's body?" I asked, puzzled.

"No. If he threw him overboard, it'll take a while before he resurfaces. The police consider the case to be almost closed. We'll be able to dock out as soon as they've secured all the evidence from the suite."

19

APRIL 2014

I was shocked, to put it mildly. My dad and I agreed to meet up in an hour to go for dinner. I walked back to my suite and locked the door behind me. Victor still had his nose in Christoffer's book and I wondered if he had even noticed that I was gone. Christoffer looked up and I smiled.

"It's nothing. Just some technical issue they need to fix," I lied, so he wouldn't be scared. I wasn't going to ruin his trip with this.

Christoffer returned to his TV show. I sat down, feeling slightly fearful. I couldn't believe I had been so close to this guy. I had seen his anger in full display. I was just glad he hadn't pulled the gun while I had still been in the room. It was scary to know a man like that had been right down the hallway from us.

"Is it okay Victor is reading your book?" I asked Christoffer.

He nodded. "Yeah. It's really boring."

"But you let him know if you need it, alright? Your teacher told you to read it on your trip."

"I know," Christoffer said. He turned off the TV and walked to his room and closed the door.

I went to the minibar and found a light beer. I opened it and drank.

Suddenly, Victor lifted his eyes from the book and looked out the window. It had gotten dark outside.

"She killed herself," he said.

"What was that?" I asked.

"That lady you saved. She killed herself. That's why we're not leaving."

"No. You've got it wrong. Her husband shot her," I said. "I was just out there. The police arrested the husband."

But Victor didn't listen to what I said.

"She was upset because of her son," he said. "She felt guilty. She knew he was dead. She knew that he had died. So she wanted to die too. She couldn't bear to wait for someone to tell her she was right."

"No, Victor. The husband killed her. He tried to make it look like a suicide. You've got it all wrong."

"He didn't like guns. It was her gun," Victor mumbled.

"So what? He could have shot her with her own gun," I said, feeling tired and not wanting to go on with this conversation. I was, quite frankly, a little freaked out.

"No gunshot residue," Victor said, right before his eyes returned to the book.

I didn't take much notice of what he said and turned on the TV. I grabbed another light beer and drank it. A little later, my dad knocked on my door.

"Are you guys ready to get something to eat?" he asked.

We walked downstairs and ate a nice dinner at one of the ship's many restaurants, then returned to our deck where two officers were waiting for me in front of my suite.

"Mrs. Frost?" They said with a heavy Italian accent to their English. "We need to ask you a few questions."

I invited them inside. I put Victor to bed and asked Christoffer to get himself ready, then tucked him in as well before I returned to the living room where they were sitting.

"It won't take long, Mrs. Frost," one of the officers said.

"That's okay. I'm not going anywhere," I said. "I just didn't want the kids to hear anything."

"Of course not. As you probably know, this is regarding the Colombos. We understand you spent some time with them yesterday?"

"Well, I did. Mrs. Colombo was in trouble. She had passed out because she had forgotten to eat. She was diabetic. So I called for a doctor and he took care of it. Really, I didn't do much."

"We've already spoken to the doctor. But, as we understand it, Mr. and Mrs. Colombo had a...uhm, a quarrel while you were both present. Is that true?"

"Yes. They were concerned about their son. He had been missing for a long time and they were worried. I think most couples would be fighting."

"We're not here to judge, Mrs. Frost. We just take notes of the facts," the other officer said.

"Did Mr. Colombo seem threatening to you?" the first officer asked.

"What do you mean by threatening?" I asked. I was beginning to feel a little uncomfortable. I didn't like to add more to the case against Alonzo Colombo. A thought had entered my mind, put there by Victor.

What if he was innocent?

"Was he being threatening towards Mrs. Colombo?" the officer continued.

I exhaled. I had to tell them the truth. "Well. He was angry. That was very obvious," I said diplomatically.

"We've been told that he threw a lamp against the wall and shattered it. Is this true?"

I nodded, seeing all the headlines in the newspapers before my eyes. I exhaled. I had to tell them what I saw.

"That is the truth, yes. He threw the lamp."

"Thank you so much, Mrs. Frost. That was all we wanted to know," the first officer said and got up from the couch. "Enjoy the rest of your cruise."

20

APRIL 2014

I didn't feel good about myself once the officers had left. I didn't quite understand why I felt this way, since I had seen the man yell at his wife and act with great anger. There was no reason for me to think he was innocent.

Except for what Victor said.

I sighed and grabbed another beer from the mini-bar. What did Victor even know about this case? He hadn't been with me in the room. He didn't see how angry Alonzo Colombo was at his wife.

But he did know that the wife needed a doctor. He did know that she was dead before you told him anything.

I shook my head and turned on the TV in my suite. After all, I had only told the officers the truth. They already knew he had thrown that lamp from the doctor's statement. Nothing I said could change their minds about Mr. Colombo anyway.

I switched the channel. An old episode of *Friends* was on. It was in Italian. I watched it anyway. I knew what it was about. It was the one where Chandler decided to try and commit to a relationship with Janice and screwed it all up by getting too clingy and needy. I didn't understand much of what they said, but it didn't matter. I just needed something to take my mind off the murder. I knew it would be hard for me to sleep.

Chandler was eating ice cream with Monica and Rachel when I went for some chocolate from the mini-bar. I ate it all, but it didn't make me feel any better. I looked out the big windows leading to my balcony and wondered if we would be able to depart at midnight as promised. It was pitch dark outside, nothing but the endless ocean. I thought about my home and my family. I had to admit, I was actually pretty stoked about my parents getting back together again.

I walked outside on the balcony and felt the warm spring breeze. There were voices coming from the other balconies surrounding me. It made me feel safe. I drew in a deep breath of the salty air and closed my eyes. I thought about my childhood back in my old house in Elsinore where I grew up in an average middle-class Danish home. My parents had been annoyingly normal and my childhood very uneventful. I guessed that was part of why I had felt so compelled to act out greatly as a teenager. I had cut my hair into a Mohawk, colored it green and worn military boots and lots of piercings. I laughed out loud, thinking about it. What a shocker it must have been for my parents. Their pretty daughter suddenly becoming rebellious like that. I even, at one time, had a chain from my earring to my nose-piercing. It must have scared them. Even scarier was the crowd I started to hang out with in Copenhagen. Every weekend, I took off to the capitol and hung out with these people who fought for anarchy in our country, occupied houses, and demonstrated against the government in the streets. We were quite the bunch. I never cared much about fighting the government, but I really liked shocking my parents. And, boy, had I shocked them. I was arrested several times and they had to come and get me. I wondered how I myself would react if Maya ended up doing anything similar. I guess I would be really mad. I sipped my beer, wondering why my parents hadn't been...Why they hadn't been really angry with me for acting out like that. They had been so understanding and mellow and...well, I guess that was why I had done it. I wanted them to be outraged. I wanted them to be angry. They never were.

I thought about Maya again and felt a sort of unease inside of me. She was the exact same age now as I had been when I started acting out. Was that what she was doing now? Was it part of her rebellion? What kind of trouble would she end up getting herself into? She was so angry with me and I couldn't talk to her anymore.

I looked at my cellphone and went through all the old pictures of her and me, then felt a sadness grow inside of me. What if she never forgave me? What if she never came back? I wanted so badly to call her and tell her to come home.

But I couldn't. She needed this break from me. She needed to find her own way right now and there was nothing I could do about it.

I just had to accept it and pray she wouldn't get herself into trouble. I had to be the grown-up, the reasonable one.

God, how I hated everything about it.

21

APRIL 1980

He was making a lot of money. Officer Maraldi was practically swimming in it. Every Friday night, he took the twins to a new place in town to fight in dog fights and, every time, they won by killing the dog. It was quite the spectacle and soon the Spider Boys became famous all over the Rome underground. They came from everywhere to see them and see if it was really true that a set of circus freaks could actually kill ferocious dogs in an arena.

When they weren't fighting, he kept them in his basement. He had gotten a cage for them, so they wouldn't escape while he was at work. He couldn't risk losing his golden goose. Before a fight, he would starve them for two days, giving them nothing but dried up bread and water...Just like their opponents were starved by their owners to make them aggressive.

And the twins were growing more aggressive by the day. They would bite the bars of the cage in anger when he entered the basement and growl at him and sometimes even bark when he gave them their food.

"You're nothing but animals, aren't you?" he said, as he watched them attack the chunk of meat he brought them on the days when he wasn't starving them. He liked to watch them sink their teeth into the meat and rip it apart, growling and drooling like wild animals. He enjoyed studying them, just like everyone else who came to the shows. It was fascinating. What were they? Humans? Animals? It was impossible to tell. But as time went by, he started more and more to regard them as mere animals. Even if he still listened to them talk to each other at night, not understanding one single word.

He had bought himself a whip and a bull hook like those used to dressage big animals like elephants. With that in his hand, he didn't risk the twins attacking him when he transported them from one place to another. He had to use it a few times, but mostly to gain respect from them. Maraldi was slightly terrified of the twins, as well as fascinated. They were making him a lot of money, but he was also afraid they would cause his death some day.

He never once worried that they might be taken away from him. But that was exactly what happened. One day, when he was loading his truck after a show well-done, someone sneaked up behind him and put a gun to his face.

"Put them up," the voice said.

"I don't have any money on me," he lied.

"This is not about the money," the voice hissed.

"Then what is it about?"

A face appeared next to him. Maraldi gasped. "You!"

"Hello there, Officer Maraldi. I heard you've been looking for me," said Mama Florea, the woman known as the leader of the Slovenski Gang. She was known to be a notorious criminal who would kill any of her gang-members if they didn't bring home enough money. She wouldn't hesitate to kill him as well. Maraldi knew he had to be careful.

"What do you want?" he snorted.

"You have something that belongs to me," Mama Florea said.

"And just what might that be?" Maraldi asked. He wondered if she was talking about the money he had made tonight. It was all in the truck. He wasn't going to give it up without a fight. That was certain.

"The boys," Mama Florea said with her deep rusty voice. "Your precious Spider-boys. They're mine. I paid a lot of money for them. You've had your fun with them. Now I'm taking them home."

Maraldi's hands were shaking in anger, but he knew he had lost. It was him up against an entire gang of ruthless gypsies. He knew what they were capable of. He had seen their victims.

"So, if you don't mind, I'll just take them now and be on my way," Mama Florea said. She signaled someone and two men came forward.

"Take them," Mama Florea said.

The men did as they were told and Maraldi could do nothing but watch as his golden goose was carried away from him. Mama Florea looked at him, then smiled at the guy holding the gun.

"Now hurt him. No one steals from Mama Florea and gets away with it."

The old woman turned her back on Maraldi while the man with the gun pointed it at Maraldi's leg and pulled the trigger.

22

APRIL 2014

Francesca Alessandrino woke up when the ship took off again.

Finally, she thought to herself and looked over at her parents who were both sound asleep in the other bed.

It was past midnight and, as usual, they had all been in bed by ten-thirty. Tonight was worse than ever and they had both wanted to go to bed before ten. They demanded that all lights were out and Francesca wasn't even allowed to watch TV or play games on her iPad, since the *light from it woke them up.*

At the age of thirteen Francesca was getting increasingly more annoyed with her parents. First of all, they were too old. None of her friend's parents were this old. Her mother had been in her mid-forties when she had her and her dad was ten years older. Second, they never let her do anything fun. When her classmates went to the youth club on Friday nights, she was always told to stay home and watch old films and shows on TV with her parents.

"You don't need to be running out at night," her father said.

"It's over at ten o'clock in the evening, Dad," she had argued so many times, but it was no use.

"We never did that in my youth," her mother always said.

Maybe because you were young in the seventies!

Her parents were so extremely boring and now they had taken her on this boring cruise. It was nice and all and the suite was great, but Francesca did not appreciate the fact that she had to sleep with her parents. Both of her parents snored and she had no privacy. Her mother was always checking in on her and monitoring her time on her iPad, telling her to not spend so much time on Facebook. She would say something insanely stupid like:

"Young people today never stop to smell the flowers."

It annoyed Francesca immensely. Everything about her old parents annoyed her and sometimes she imagined running off. Just take off and live her life. She couldn't wait to be old enough to leave home.

But it was still so many years away. She wasn't sure she could wait that long. How was she supposed to survive her teenage years locked up with these old people while all her friends went to parties, drank their first beers, and hooked up with boys? It had already started. And she was already an outsider. Having to say *no, I can't come* over and over again eventually made people stop asking. Most of her friends had sympathy for her situation, but some didn't understand why she didn't just *do it anyway*. Why she didn't just sneak out at night when the old people were asleep.

"They'll never know," her friend Ada said. "They'll never find out."

But up until now, Francesca hadn't dared to do anything like that. She was afraid of her dad's anger if he found out. He always thought of her as his pretty little girl who would never get herself into trouble.

"Being the daughter of a well-known surgeon brings responsibility," he always told her.

He wanted her to go into medicine as well and she was still finding the courage to tell him it wasn't going to happen. He had retired years ago, and now he had cast all his expectations for the future upon his daughter.

"Look at those hands," he would say and grab her by the wrists. "Look at them. They're made to hold a scalpel. Look at how steady and delicate they are. They're just perfect. You are going to do great wonders in this world, my daughter."

Francesca liked that he had high hopes for her, but she knew she would never be able to live up to them. Especially not when she was dreaming about becoming a writer.

Francesca tried, once again, to fall asleep, but it was hard. She was sleeping way too much on this trip, since she had to be in bed so early. She wasn't tired at all. Finally, she got out of bed and found a pamphlet about the cruise-ship. She had heard there was a nightclub on board.

Francesca looked at her sleeping parents. The ship rocked slightly as it speeded up, probably trying to catch up from the many hours of delay.

They'll never know, she heard her friend Ada say. *They'll never find out.*

Francesca felt a thrill in her stomach as she made her decision. She went to her suitcase and found the dress she had brought with her, just in case she ever had the chance to go out. She never thought she would actually get to use it.

23

APRIL 2014

The man was happy to realize the ship was finally leaving the port. He felt the movements and heard the well-known noise from the engines close to his lower deck cabin. It was like music to his ears. That meant the police had left the ship and he could pick up his project where he had left off.

"There is much to do, Deedee," he said, while carefully placing the needle on his skin. He closed his eyes and bit down as the needle went through his shoulder.

Oh the pain. The excruciating unbearable pain.

Yet it was nothing compared to the pain he felt on the inside of him, deep within his tortured soul. Feeling the pain on his skin as he sewed through the open and infected wound made him somehow feel better. Like he was finally paying his dues.

When he was done, he looked in the mirror.

"Dashing," Deedee said.

The man tilted his head and smiled. Blood was seeping from the holes in his skin. The infected areas were pounding. But it was all worth it. Finally, he felt whole again.

"That we are."

"Busy night ahead."

"I know. Better get going." The man was sweating heavily in pain as he grabbed the long black coat from the hanger.

"I'm sorry, Deedee," he said. "I'm sorry it has to be this way."

Then he grabbed his hat and stormed out the door. The man walked up the stairs towards the upper deck, where he had long been watching the girl. This one was more than just a random donor. This one was special to him and he was really looking forward to getting his hands on her. The man had slipped the parents a sleeping pill during their dinner onboard and knew they would be heavily asleep in their suite by now. Sedated just enough for him to sneak in there and grab the girl. He had been thrilled to see her for the first time when he boarded the ship. Her dad had put his arm around her shoulder, the man remembered. But most of all, he remembered her legs. He had been thrilled to see her beautiful long legs and once he had, he knew exactly what to use her for.

"Those are a girl's legs," Deedee had protested.

But the man had thought it was perfect. Deedee was, after all, just a young boy.

The man giggled as he ran upstairs. Music came from the restaurants and bars downstairs on the ship. It was past midnight and the dancing had started. People were getting drunk. They wouldn't notice a thing. He neared the suite and rubbed his hands together in joy. Boy, how he had looked forward to this. The boy was fun, but this was a sweeter joy. It wasn't just about getting the legs on this girl. It was also about making her parents suffer.

"Make them feel the pain. Take what is dear to them like they did to you," Deedee said.

The man was looking forward to that...To seeing the suffering in their eyes when they realized they were never going to see their precious daughter again.

He stood outside the door to their suite for a few seconds, embracing the moment and preparing himself for what was about to happen when suddenly, the door opened. The man jumped aside and hid in a bathroom in the hallway. Through the door, he watched the girl silently leave the room and close the door behind her without making a sound. She was dressed in a little red dress, much too grown-up for her. The dress and the make-up made her look like she could be in her twenties. The man couldn't believe his luck.

"Going out, are we?" he mumbled with another giggle. "And without your parents knowing it? Tsk tsk! Now don't go and get yourself in trouble!"

She looked around her one more time, then stormed towards the stairs in heels that were way too high for a girl of her age. The man rubbed his fingers against each other once again. He hardly noticed the pain in his shoulder anymore. The excitement drowned it out. He was about to burst with pure delight.

Oh, how much fun this is going to be!

24

APRIL 2014

The man followed Francesca into a bar. She looked insecurely around her and tripped a little back and forth before she finally decided to sit in the bar. The man grabbed a booth behind her, so she wouldn't notice him.

Some guy came up to her and asked if he could order her a drink. She accepted and had a cocktail. The man watched her as she sipped it like an adult, while making conversation with the guy who was old enough to be her father. Soon, the guy started to bore her and she told him she had to go. The man followed her out of the bar and into a nightclub at the other end of the ship. She had a map of the ship in her hand to show her the way. The man was enjoying this little game immensely. He walked far enough behind her for her to not notice him, yet close enough to see the looks on the men's faces when she passed them. Some even turned to watch her from behind.

"It's the legs, Deedee. I tell you. Everybody loves her legs."

The girl entered the nightclub and the man followed. It was easy for him to blend into the crowd in the darkness and stay close to the girl. It was crowded in there and the music was very loud. No one asked the girl for ID. She looked old enough and, frankly, no one probably cared.

The man kept a close eye on her while she received drink after drink in the bar from strangers and danced with all of them. She seemed to be enjoying herself immensely and soon she was very, very drunk. It was clear she wasn't used to drinking.

A guy kept grabbing her behind and trying to kiss her, but she pushed him away. She went for her drink, but he grabbed her and swung her back on the dance floor. She whined, then laughed and danced with him again. The guy tried his luck again and put his lips on hers, but she slapped him across the face. The guy then slapped her back. So hard she fell onto the floor. People around them were too drunk to notice what was going on and no one reacted when the guy slapped the girl once again and yelled at her.

"Don't you ever do that again!"

Then he grabbed her arm and, while she was sobbing and slightly confused, he pulled her up and out of the club. The man followed. Outside the nightclub, the guy pulled Francesca by the arm and, even though she protested, she was forced to go with him. She was too drunk to know what was really going on.

"Where are you taking me?" she asked, talking slowly and sounding suddenly like the child she was.

"You're coming with me. I have been paying drinks for you all night, little girl. Now I'll have my way with you. It's payback time. I'm guessing a young girl like you haven't exactly told her parents where she is, so if you don't want me to tell them, you better do everything I tell you to. Everything."

Francesca whimpered. "But...But...I'm only thirteen. I've never..."

"You're thirteen, huh?" the guy said. "Well, I like them young." He pulled her aside then brought her outside on the empty deck of the ship. He placed her in a corner and put his hand over her mouth. He pulled up her dress and put his hand up under it.

"Oh yes. You sure are young. A virgin, huh? Well, it's my lucky day. Virgins are my FAVORITES!"

"Please don't," Francesca pleaded. She was crying now. No one could hear her because of the winds and the roaring ocean.

The man was watching the spectacle from a distance, smoking a cigarette. The guy was all over Francesca, licking her ears and neck and groping her with his big hands.

"Please don't do this," Francesca sobbed.

"I'll do exactly as I please. Just you wait and see," the guy said, moaning with arousal.

"No. No. I'll do anything. Just not this."

"Shut up!" the guy said and slapped Francesca across the face again. Now she was crying heavily.

"Stop it. Stop hitting me."

The guy hit her again. This time, with his fist in her face. Then he turned her around and leaned her up against the wall. He pulled her dress further up. "Slut," he hissed and pulled his own pants down. He put his hand over her mouth and whispered.

"Now I'm gonna make you a woman."

Just as he was about to enter her, the man stepped forward and placed his cigarette butt in the guy's right eye. The guy screamed and cupped it.

"Aaaargh! My eye! My eye!"

"Step away from the girl, you freaking bastard. Step away from her. NOW!"

The guy staggered back and forth yelling all kinds of atrocities at the man. He walked backwards towards the railing and came very close to it, when the man reached out his arm and pushed him over it.

25

APRIL 2014

"**A**RGH!?"

Francesca screamed and ran towards the railing. She spotted the guy she had met in the club right before he hit the water and became quiet. Then she shrieked and turned to look at the man who had been her savior.

"Wha...What happened?" she asked, with a trembling voice. She hadn't seen what happened after he was burned with the cigarette. She had covered her face, thinking he would hit her again and, when she looked again, the guy was suddenly gone. "Where...where did he go? Did he...?"

The man lit another cigarette and nodded while blowing out smoke. "Yes, Francesca," he said. "He fell overboard. These things happen when you're drunk and not careful. He won't bother you again." The man smoked and tilted his head. "Now, there Francesca. Don't cry. There's no need to cry."

Francesca tried to hold back her tears and ended up sobbing. "It's just... It...I...I was so scared. And now he's...he fell, you said?"

"Yes, Francesca. He walked backwards and fell overboard. He was drunk. These things happen."

"I think he was...I think he was going to rape me. If you hadn't shown up...," Francesca stuttered.

"Yes, I know. I saw it all. You really should be more careful."

"Did he really fall?" she asked again. "Shouldn't we tell someone? Shouldn't we tell the captain and have him stop the ship or something?"

The man finished his cigarette and threw it in the water. "Don't you worry your pretty little head about that. I'll take care of it. Now, let's not think any more about him. My dear, are you alright? You still seem a little shaken."

"I...I think I'm alright. My cheek hurts though," Francesca said. She lifted her hand and touched her nose. It was bleeding. "Oh my God," she said. "I must look awful. I can't go back to my parents looking like this. They'll know I snuck out and got myself into trouble. They'll never let me leave the house again. I'm going to be a prisoner for the rest of my teenage years."

Francesca started crying again. The man reached into his pocket and pulled out a package of Kleenex. "Don't cry. Here wipe your eyes. I might be able to help you."

She sniffled and looked up at him with her big brown eyes. "Really? You can help me?"

"Yes. I might. We need to stop the bleeding first, then I can cover most of the bruises with make-up. I work in theater and have a foundation that can cover anything. But it's all back in my cabin. Let me go get it."

Francesca grabbed his arm. "Don't leave me here. Please let me go with you. I don't want to be alone. Not after what happened."

She could have sworn she saw a small creepy smile grow on his face.

You're just being paranoid, Francesca. Just because one guy was mean to you doesn't mean every guy you meet will be. This man actually saved your life.

"Okay," the man said. "Then follow me."

Francesca smiled and they walked arm in arm inside the ship and continued towards the stairs. Francesca felt so secure with this man and leaned her head on one of his shoulders like she always did on her dad's.

She was still bleeding from the nose as they reached the lower deck. She held her head back and covered the nostrils with the paper towel like the man had told her to, while he found his keycard and slid it through. He opened the door and held it for her.

"Ladies first."

Francesca giggled. She had never been treated like this or been called *a lady* before. She walked inside his nice little cabin and the door shut behind them. The cabin wasn't as big as her parent's suite, but it wasn't as small as she had feared either. It had a living room and a bedroom. But no windows. Only wooden paneling all over, making it a little dark and old fashioned.

"This is nice," she said, but didn't really mean it. It wasn't bad, but there was just something about this place that was a little...well, she didn't have the words for it.

"Sit down on the couch," the man said and pointed at a small brown couch. Francesca sat down.

The man smiled. "I'll get my things. They're in the bedroom. Don't forget to lean your head backwards. Your nose is still bleeding."

Francesca held her napkin to her nose again and leaned her head back.

"Be right back," the man said.

Francesca nodded without looking at him. He went into the bedroom and left her alone. Francesca was getting a sore neck from holding her head in this position, so she let her head drop for a second when her eyes suddenly spotted something in the small living room. There was something pinned to the walls in front of her. What was that? Polaroid pictures? She got up and walked towards them. She looked at them one after another, while gasping. She stumbled backwards with her heart thudding in her chest.

"I got it," a voice said from behind her.

She shrieked and turned. She looked directly into the man's face.

"You like my photos?" he asked. The creepy smile was back.

"What...who...what is that?" she stuttered with fear.

"My work, you like it?"

"I...I...what is it?"

"Oh. You want to meet him? Of course. Where are my manners? You should meet him. I'm so sorry," the man said. He grabbed the black coat and pulled it off.

"Deedee meet Francesca. Francesca meet Deedee."

26

APRIL 2014

I woke up around two o'clock because I thought I heard someone screaming very loudly. But when I opened my eyes, the sound was already gone.

Was it just a dream?

I looked over at Victor, who was in my bed. Then I shrieked. Victor was awake and sitting up. He was looking directly at me.

"Victor, goddammit. Don't scare me like that!"

He didn't say anything.

"Are you alright? Was it you I heard screaming? Did you have another nightmare?"

Victor didn't react to anything I did or said. He sat completely still.

"Victor? Are you alright? Oh my God. You're shivering."

I reached over and turned on the lights on the wall. I looked at my son. His eyes were open, but he didn't seem like he was awake. He didn't seem to be looking at anything. Just that blank stare that completely freaked me out.

"What's wrong, Victor? Did you dream something?"

Suddenly, I spotted something under his nose. "Is that blood?" I found a paper napkin and wiped it away. More was coming from his nose. "Victor.

You're bleeding. Lean your head backwards and hold this to stop the blood." I placed another paper napkin in his hand, but he didn't hold on to it. It fell onto the bed.

"Victor!" I was almost crying now. "Victor. You've got to wake up. You're bleeding from your nose."

The door to Christoffer's room opened and he came out in his PJs. "What's going on?"

"Victor is just having a bad dream," I said.

Christoffer came closer. "Is he bleeding?" he asked, terrified.

"Just a little nosebleed," I moaned, trying hard not to freak out and scare the boy.

"I'll get some more tissues," Christoffer said. He went into the bathroom then returned with a box of Kleenex. He pulled one out and held it on Victor's nose, gently wiping the blood off. I was moved.

"It's not so bad," he said with a calm voice. "My sister Ida gets nosebleed all the time. It's not as bad as hers. But he has to keep his head back."

"I know," I said.

Suddenly, Victor looked at me. His face was expressionless. His lips were moving, but I couldn't hear what he was saying. I moved closer and realized he was singing, muttering the words under his breath.

"Tweedledum and Tweedledee agreed to have a battle. For Tweedledum said Tweedledee had spoiled his nice new rattle. Just then flew down a monstrous crow, as black as a tar-barrel, which frightened both the heroes so, they quite forgot their quarrel."

"Victor you're really scaring me here. Please snap out of it," I said and snapped my fingers in the air, thinking the sound would wake him from this trance.

"It's the rhyme from the book," Christoffer said.

"What?" I asked.

"Lewis Carroll's *Through the Looking-Glass*. The twins...Tweedledum and Tweedledee. Alice recites the rhyme when she meets the twins," Christoffer said.

"Maybe I should call the doctor," I said.

I reached over to get the phone and dial the receptionist's number when suddenly Victor's body seemed to relax and fall backwards. I put the phone down and walked over to him. The blood had stopped and his eyes were now closed. I leaned over to listen to his breath. He was breathing normally.

Christoffer shrugged. "I guess he fell back asleep. I think I'll go back to my room then."

With my heart still pounding in my chest, I sat on the bed and stared at Victor for almost an hour before I finally decided to go back to sleep.

The next morning, Victor seemed just like he usually did. There was no more bleeding and no more weird staring. We ate breakfast on the balcony while the ship was cruising the Mediterranean Sea. We weren't going to be in Sicily until the next morning, according to the plan, and with the delay from yesterday, we were probably going to arrive very late. Hopefully we would be there at lunchtime, so there still was time to explore the island. There was only scheduled sightseeing for one day before the ship left Italy and moved on to Malta.

My mom and dad joined us later and we ate together. It made me feel good...To have my family close like this. Well, most of it anyway. I couldn't stop thinking about Maya and how I would have loved to have her with us.

"So what are you guys up to today?" my dad asked.

"I was thinking we'd explore the ship a little. Maybe hit the pool on the upper deck later on. Have a cocktail and lie in the sun. What about you?"

"I'd love to go in the pool," Christoffer said. "You want to come with me, Victor?"

Victor nodded without looking up.

"Same here," my dad said. "Your mother wants to look at the stores on the middle deck. There's a Victoria's Secret that she wants us to explore. Then we'll hit the pool as well."

I chuckled. My mom looked at me.

"What? I can't dress in nice lingerie for my husband just because I'm old?"

"No. No. I mean, of course you can. That's none of my business. It's just really hard to picture your mother...never mind," I said, emptied my coffee and finished my croissant.

"We'll probably join you at the pool around noon," my dad continued. "Maybe we should have lunch up there? I hear there's a restaurant that serves the best seafood while you overlook the ocean."

"Sounds like a plan," I said and smiled. I looked at Victor, who was reading his book at the table. The night's strange events still lingered with me and gave me an eerie feeling, but I decided to shake it and move on.

"Meet you at the pool in about two hours, then?" My dad said and got up from his chair.

"See you then."

27

APRIL 2014

Exploring the ship wasn't too much fun with Victor. He didn't want to go into any of the shops and didn't like the many people constantly crowding everywhere we went. I should have known. He never liked being among a lot of people. I still dragged him and Christoffer through all the stores aboard and ended up buying Christoffer a truck and Victor a book about Pompeii, just to make it up to them. Also, I hoped Victor would stop reading the other book that apparently had made a little too great of an impression on him and given him the nightmares.

Once he got the book, he went silent. He studied the pictures and indulged himself in the stories, while I tried on dresses and bought all kinds of knick-knacks for Maya that I knew she was never going to like. I bought a new cologne for Morten and a very expensive shirt.

When I had enough, we went back to the suite and placed all the bags in the living room, then found our swimsuits and put them on. Victor didn't seem as thrilled to go as Christoffer. It wasn't that he didn't like to go swimming. As a matter of fact, he loved to swim. It was one of the few sports he really enjoyed. No, he was worried about the amount of people and other children in and around the pool. He was worried about how crowded and loud they were going to be. He liked his space and he was very sensitive to loud sounds.

"You ready?" I asked, when he came out from the bathroom in his new swim shorts that I had just bought him. "They look great on you, buddy. They fit just perfect, huh?"

"Yeah, Victor," Christoffer said. "I can't wait to get in the pool. It's huge. There's a waterslide and everything."

I grabbed my bag with sunscreen and towels and a book for myself and opened the door. Victor walked out, while hugging his new book, holding it to his chest like he was afraid someone was going to steal it from him. I was glad I had found something that made him happy and taken his eyes off of Lewis Carroll's *Through the Looking-Glass.* It was back in Christoffer's room where it belonged.

We found a nice spot by the pool and I was thrilled to see that we were among the first there. Only three other children were playing in the children's area. An older couple was swimming laps. A woman was enjoying the sun, while her husband seemed to be annoyed to be there.

Victor and Christoffer jumped in the pool and I threw my body in a lounger pretending to read my book, but really dozing off. I hadn't slept much after the strange incident with Victor. I woke up when Victor came running towards me and sat on my chair with his wet shorts.

"Huh?" I said and opened my eyes. I smiled when I saw Victor sitting at the foot of my chair. "Did you have fun?"

He nodded and sniffled. I felt good. The nap helped. Christoffer waved from the top of the slide. I waved back.

"There you are."

I lifted my head and looked at my dad who was standing next to me, flanked by my mother in a very expensive-looking bathing suit. Her body still looked amazing after all the work she had done, except now she had some scars on her thighs where they had taken the skin that they used to repair her face. My dad had his arm around her. He looked more like an ordinary Dane. A little overweight with very, very pale legs. He was wearing socks with his sandals.

"So, did you get some shopping done?" I asked.

"Well, it was hard with all the people," my mother said and sat down on the lounge chair next to mine. "They were looking for a girl, you know."

"No. I didn't know. What girl is that?"

"Some teenager who was last seen dancing at one of the nightclubs last night. She was very drunk, they all say, and left with some guy. They can't find him either. They fear that they both might have fallen overboard. The parents are freaking out. I saw them on the upper deck talking to the captain when we went back with our stuff. They actually live in the suite right next to ours. Mr. and Mrs. Alessandrino. I talked to them briefly. They said the girl never went out at night. That she was in her bed when they went to sleep last night. But surveillance cameras from the nightclub show her dancing with this guy. It's all very strange."

"Ah, it's nothing," my dad said. "They probably got too drunk and ended up crashing somewhere. They'll both turn up later today. Just wait and see."

I looked at Victor who was sitting very still while drops of water dripped on my lounge-chair. I wondered if he knew anything...If him waking up in the middle of the night had anything to do with the disappearance of the two.

"Well, we said the same about Alberto Colombo, didn't we?" I asked. "We thought he'd show up too. And he didn't. He hasn't been found yet."

"That's different," my dad said. "The dad went nuts and killed both of them. He's not onboard anymore."

I grunted, dissatisfied. I didn't like this one bit. Something was very wrong on this boat.

"Photo?"

I looked up through my sunglasses and spotted a man in a black jacket. He was holding a Polaroid camera between his hands.

"Excuse me?" I asked.

"Would you like to have your photo taken with your beautiful family?"

"Yes," my mother burst out. She turned to look at my dad and continued in Danish to him. "Wouldn't we dear? I would love to have a picture of all of us from this great vacation."

I stared at the man with the old camera. Who used Polaroid cameras in these days of digital cameras? I wondered. It was odd.

"I don't know, Ulla," my dad growled. "I mean, we're in our swimsuits and everything."

"Ah, come on papa-bear. I saw this guy at the restaurant last night," my mother continued. "Ever since I saw him take a picture of another family, I've wanted to get one for ourselves. But, when I wanted to catch him, he was gone. Do it for me. You too Emma. And Victor. And Christoffer, of course," she said and waved at him to come. He sprang towards us. My mother looked up at the photographer and spoke in English to him.

"Take one of all of us."

We all sat very close, surrounding Victor and Christoffer in the middle. The man lifted his camera. "Smile," he said. "Say cheese."

We all smiled and the camera clicked. Then Victor burst into a high-pitched scream. He clapped his ears with both hands and simply screamed. The photographer seemed startled.

"I'm sorry," he said.

"It's not your fault. Victor is a very sensitive boy," I said.

"Okay," the photographer said. He pulled out the photo and let it dry in the air, while I tried to get Victor to calm down. When nothing else helped, I found his book and put it in his lap on a towel, so it wouldn't get wet. Victor immediately stopped screaming. My mom paid the photographer, who took off in a hurry. Christoffer jumped back in the pool.

"You really should learn to control that boy," my mother said. "That was embarrassing."

"He can't help it, Mom. He probably got scared from a sound or something."

"There was no sound," my mother said. "I tell you, that boy isn't normal."

"Ulla, the boy has a condition," my dad started defending me.

"Thank you, Dad. The thing is, we never know why he reacts the way he does. It might be something in his imagination, or maybe he just didn't want to have his picture taken."

"Well then, he should learn to say so. Learn to use his words instead of just screaming. Scared me half to death," my mother snorted.

"Well, it is part of what we're working on with him. We're working with this guy now, trying to teach him some social skills. But Rome wasn't built in a day, Mom. These things take time. And he will never be normal, if that's what you're waiting for," I had to pause to calm myself down. I was getting all worked up. I knew my mother always had a hard time understanding Victor's condition and I often felt like she thought I was the problem.

"Let's get something to eat," my dad said. "I, for one, am starving."

"Me too," I said. "Christoffer! Get out of the pool. We're leaving for lunch now."

As usual, food was our solution to a conflict in my family. It had been for as long as I could remember.

28

APRIL 1982

The twins were back with the gypsies, who were now the ones that were making a lot of money off of them. Not by having them fight vicious dogs like the police officer had, but by showing them off in the street...in a tent where people had to pay to see the creatures that no one knew whether they were humans or animals.

They had taken them on the road. Living in the back of their trucks. Every day they were in a new town where they would put up their show. And every day, before their show, the gypsies beat up the twins with sticks —not to make them look poor and pitiful like earlier—but to make them angry and aggressive. They put a chain around their necks and tied them up and poked them in the stomach to make them bark and growl at the people.

"Come and see the beast," A man standing outside the tent yelled. "It's as ferocious and ruthless as anything you've ever seen. See it before it kills again. Is it a giant two-headed spider? Is it a monstrous dog? Or are they savages, wild humans ready to attack at any moment you're not paying attention. Come and see for yourself. See the beast. Hear it growl. Watch it as it thirsts for your blood."

The twins were getting increasingly afraid of humans and especially of getting beaten with the sticks, so they did as they were told. They growled and writhed their body, making it look like they were trying to get loose, trying to attack the spectators. They had lost their Italian language, forgotten it since it was never used. Now they only had their mutual language in between them, but even that, they never used anymore, since they almost never spoke to one another. But even if they tried to yell for help, no one understood anything they would say or yell. When they spoke, people laughed and clapped their hands. Some even yelled profanities back at them. They called them names and spat at them.

Creeps.

Freaks.

Monsters.

Mutants.

"Look at their sharp teeth," the gypsies would yell. "Look at their claws. Don't stand too close to them. Those teeth will go straight through your skin and they'll suck your blood, suck you dry till there is no more left."

The crowd then gasped and pulled away with big eyes and open mouths.

"See what happens when I poke it with my stick, the presenter would say. Then he poked the twins in the stomach and they reacted with a huge roar. The crowd gasped again in fear and fascination. Then the presenter swung the stick and hurt the twins so they whimpered, pulling backwards.

"Down!" he yelled.

The crowd clapped and cheered. It was always the same. Every day for eight hours a day. A new crowd every hour. Once the twins returned to their cage in the back of the truck, they were exhausted...beaten and humiliated enough to crumple up in a corner and not speak a word to one another. They hardly ate and soon became very skinny...Something that made them even scarier to look at.

It wasn't until one night when they were back in Rome after two years on the road that they finally spoke to one another again. The gypsies had parked the truck in a parking lot close to the place they had chosen for their show later in the day. Everyone else was sleeping heavily when the twins both opened their eyes at the same second, like had it been synchronized, or had been planned in advance. For the first time in a long while, they looked into each other's eyes.

"Today, we are twelve years old," one of them said in their mutual language.

"Today, we take back our lives," the other replied.

"I love you."

"I love you more."

29

APRIL 2014

"What are you doing? I can't see."

"Don't be impatient, Deedee," the man said. "I don't want to rush this. I want it to be perfect."

"I can't wait. Could you do something about this smell soon? I can't stand this smell," Deedee complained.

"You know that's my next move."

The man moaned and wiped off drops of sweat from his forehead. He was concentrating very hard right now. Carefully, he sewed the pieces of skin together. On the floor, in a black plastic garbage bag, lay the remains of the girl. She was missing an entire leg, cut off at the points directly below the groin. On the back and front of her chest, the man had cut off big pieces of her skin.

She hadn't suffered. The man didn't want her to. No, she wasn't the one who needed to feel pain. Her parents were. It was never the man's intention to have her feel any pain. He had slit her throat in one quick movement as soon as she started screaming. That had shut her up immediately. Blood had gushed onto the floor and he had hurried to put her body into the plastic bag. He would have to clean up the blood later.

He carried her inside the bag into the bathroom, where he had hung her from her feet inside the shower. With a long-bladed knife, he had cut up her dead body. He started at one corner of the jaw and made a deep ear-to-ear cut through the neck and larynx to the opposite side. This severed the internal and external carotid arteries, the major blood vessels carrying blood from the heart to the head, face, and brain. He had let her hang for a while...Draining her blood and letting it all wash out with the bathwater. Then he had cleaned the skin carefully.

The man had carried the dead body back into the living room of his cabin, then thrown her on another plastic bag so he wouldn't leave traces on the floor. First he cut off the leg, then later, with a scalpel, he started flaying her in certain spots where he knew the skin was best. Then he had started sewing it.

"Hurry up. Hurry up," Deedee said.

"Patience, mio caro."

The man turned to face the girl again. He kneeled next to her and examined her skin. He found a great spot on her stomach and, with a scalpel, he cut it off. The finest skin was found on the back and abdomen. He was careful to just get the skin. The skin was composed of two layers, an outer thinner one with a thicker tissue layer below it. He only needed the outer layer. Carefully and precisely, he flayed the pieces he needed. Then, he cleaned the piece of skin of blood and meat in the bathroom and sterilized it. Then he went back to his needle and thread. With a strong wrist and firm hand, he put the needle through the skin and sewed the piece onto another one.

"What are you doing now?" Deedee asked.

"I've finished the leg. Now I'm repairing the other one. It needs new skin. The old one started to rot."

"I know. I can smell it," Deedee said.

"We'll fix it," the man said. "I'll fix it. Just trust me."

"I trust you," Deedee said.

The man walked to Deedee's case and held his creation up in front of him. "See? I'm almost done. Just need to make sure it fits. It's like pants. I made it like pants so you can put them on."

"It looks great," Deedee said. "Help me get it on."

The man placed the leg in the case, then stuffed the bones that once were another leg, into the human-skin pants.

"There," he said, with tears in his voice. "It's perfect."

"Now I have two legs like everyone else," Deedee said.

The man nodded. "Yes, you do."

"I'm the luckiest boy in the world."

"Yes, you are. You're just like all the other boys."

"It's perfect," Deedee said

The man nodded, while holding back his tears. He grabbed his camera. "Smile, Deedee. Smile."

30

APRIL 2014

Victor had a hard time calming down after the photograph incident by the pool. He was restless at lunch in the restaurant and couldn't sit still on his chair. I couldn't shake what my mother had said and tried to calm him, constantly telling him to sit still. It created an annoying tension between all of us at the table. I couldn't help feeling that my mother was comparing the two boys and thinking, why couldn't Victor be more like Christoffer, who sat nicely at the table and ate quietly?

My dad tried to ease the tension by talking about food and what we were eating. I ordered a huge seafood platter and ate everything, but I couldn't really enjoy it, since I was way too tense.

"I think I'll take the boys back to the suite now," I said, when I'd finished my last shrimp. "Victor needs his rest. There's too much noise and too many people everywhere."

"Arh, come on," my mom said. "It's not too bad, is it?"

If only looks could kill.

"Well, it is to him. A nap will do him good."

"I thought we were hanging out by the pool after lunch," my mom said. "I was looking forward to spending some time with my grandchild in the water."

"Now, Ulla. If the boy needs his rest...," my dad said.

"You're always taking her side against me," my mom interrupted him. "Why is that? You're all ganging up on me. I feel like I don't really belong in this family anymore," my mom sniffled.

I rolled my eyes. She was playing the victim-card again. I wasn't falling for it. But my dad was.

"No. No. Ulla. That's not true. Of course you're a part of the family, just as much as the rest of us."

"Just because I've been away for a little while, doesn't mean I don't love all of you," she said, sobbing.

It was ridiculous. Her little charade was too much for me.

"Of course not," my dad said. "Emma tell her."

I frowned. "Tell her what? That it doesn't matter that she was gone for almost five years of her children's lives? That she missed some of the most important days of her grandchildren's lives? Well, I can't. Because it's not true. It does matter. It matters a great deal."

My mother gasped and held her chest. "How can you say such horrible things Emma?"

"Because it's the truth. It's how I feel. I know you're back and I love that you and Dad are doing so well. It's truly amazing, but you can't come back and pretend like you haven't been away. You can't come here and be condescending towards me because I have a son who is a little different and might not be the perfect grandson you wanted. Yes, he is different. But he is also smart and a great kid. And I happen to be doing this the best way I know how to. You can't just come here after all this time and think you know anything about how he should be treated. You don't know him, Mom. You don't know anything about us."

My mother sighed and gesticulated, resigned. "Okay. So I was gone. So I don't know much about what has been going on with you. What do you want from me? I'm trying here, Emma. I'm trying to get back in your life, but you won't let me."

"No, you're not, Mom. You're not even trying to get to know us again. You never ask about anything. You never asked me about my divorce or how it affected Victor and Maya. You never asked about how it has been for me to have to raise a kid with several diagnoses for mental illnesses, what it has been like to run from doctor to doctor only to get more confused and have no real answers. If you're so interested in us, like you claim to be, you would at least ask me how I've been."

My mom snorted again, then sipped her white wine with tight lips. I felt a knot in my stomach. I hated conflicts. I hated fights. My dad did too. He looked insecure and very, very uncomfortable. He was squirming in his chair and sweating heavily.

"Now, anyone up for dessert?" he asked. "I hear they make a killer Tiramisu. I always wanted to try the real thing in a real Italian restaurant."

I scoffed, leaned over and kissed my dad on the forehead. "Nothing for me, Dad. I need to get Victor back. Come on boys. We're leaving."

31

APRIL 2014

I was exhausted from the fight when I got back to the upper deck. Victor had calmed down a little now and was trotting along behind me, while flipping pages in his book. I felt horrible. Especially for Christoffer, for coming into the middle of all this. Part of me wanted to go back and apologize to my mother, but the other part was happy that I had told her those things. It was, after all, the truth. It was hard for me to let her into my life again, since I was still so angry with her for leaving. It wasn't something that simply passed after a few days together. It was a deep-rooted anger that was eating me up inside.

I called Morten from my room, while Victor and Christoffer watched a show on the TV. I walked on the balcony and talked with him for almost an hour. It helped a lot. Morten could do that. He could always make me feel better.

"Thank you for being there," I said, when I was about to hang up.

"No problem. Things are pretty boring around here with you guys out of town anyway, so I have all the time in the world."

"Yeah, I wish I could say the same about this place. It's crazy. Well, I better get going. Talk to you later?"

"Absolutely."

I threw myself on the couch next to Victor, who was watching some strange documentary again on the History Channel. This time it was showing some forensic investigator working on a murder case. The story was quite macabre. It was all in English, but I sensed Victor understood a lot of it anyway. He did take English in school, so that was probably why.

I found my iPad and opened Facebook. I scrolled through my friend's updates and soon concluded nothing much was happening in their lives. I opened a Danish news site and read some news updates and soon concluded that nothing much had happened there. But there was one article that made me stop and read. It was the story about the race driver Alonzo Colombo, who was now detained by the police and accused of having murdered his wife and son on a cruise ship along the Italian coast. The article went through the events as the police believed they had taken place onboard the ship. And then the things that puzzled them. For one, they hadn't found the body of the son yet. They had searched the waters at the harbor of Sorrento with divers and boats, but found nothing. They knew Alonzo Colombo had left the ship on the day of the son's disappearance and been away most of the day. Unlike the other passengers aboard, he and his wife hadn't gone on the trip to Mount Vesuvius and Pompeii. He had taken a rented limo and gone to visit friends of his who were vacationing in the town in a place up a great hill. They had searched the house and the cliffs and waters beneath it, but found no trace of the boy.

"It's all very strange," a police inspector was quoted saying. "It's our theory that he must have dumped the body somewhere in the city to hide his actions. Maybe his wife was even in on it. Maybe that was why he had to kill her, as well, later on. But we're not giving up. We will keep on looking. The body will show up sooner or later."

Until then, they were focusing on charging the race-driver with killing his wife. But there was another detail that puzzled the officer. The fact that Alonzo Colombo had no gunshot residue on his hands or any part of his body when they took him in. He hadn't taken a shower, there was still some of his wife's blood on his shirt from the blow. All the investigation of the crime scene seemed to benefit the race-driver's explanation.

"We still believe he's guilty," the inspector said. "There is no doubt about it. We just need to find more evidence to prove it."

I put my iPad down and looked outside. There wasn't a cloud in the sky. It was a beautiful day.

No gunshot residue, huh?

I turned my head and looked at Victor. Then I thought about what he had told me. He knew this. Somehow he knew this.

The question was, what else did he know? Did this have anything to do with his nightmares? With his sudden nosebleed? Could Alonzo Colombo be innocent? Was it possible?

I thought about the girl who had disappeared last night. If Alonzo Colombo was, in fact, innocent, then that would mean someone else had made Alberto Colombo disappear. It would also mean that that someone was still on this ship.

I got up from the couch and looked at Victor and Christoffer. "I need to go talk to someone, guys. Just stay here and watch your show."

32

APRIL 2014

I walked out into the hallway. I walked to the right towards my parents' suite, then knocked on the door to the one next to theirs. An older woman opened the door. She looked weary.

"*Sì?*"

"Mrs. Alessandrino?" I asked in English.

"That's me."

"Can I come in? My name is Emma Frost. My parents are your neighbors. I'm staying in a suite further down the hallway."

The woman looked confused, then opened the door and let me in.

"Thank you," I said and walked past her inside their suite.

In the living room, I found Mr. Alessandrino. He was sitting in a chair, looking glum and worried.

"We have a guest, Michael," Mrs. Alessandrino said in English. "Her name is Emma Frost."

"Hello, Mr. Alessandrino," I said.

He didn't answer. He kept staring out at the moving ocean. "If she fell in the water, then we're just moving further and further away from her every minute," he said. "We asked if they could stop and go back, but they said it was too late. The coastguard is out there, looking for her and that guy. All we can do is sit here and wait. Wait for what, I ask? Wait till they pull her dead body out of the water? Wait for them to knock on this door and tell us we were right? I know she's dead. I just know it in my father's heart. It's all in here, you know," he said, and punched his chest hard. "My heart is bleeding right now. It is hurting so bad. I'd rather jump in that water myself and look for her. I might die, but at least that would be something. At least I wouldn't be sitting here."

I felt Mrs. Alessandrino's hand on my arm. "You have to excuse Dr. Alessandrino. He was...is very close with our daughter. She has always been a daddy's girl. Please have a seat."

I sat at the dining table. Their suite was a little bigger than mine and had a formal dining room as well.

"I'm sorry I can't get you anything," the woman said, almost bursting into tears at the fact.

"It's okay. I didn't come here to be served. I came here to see if I could be of help to you."

Mrs. Alessandrino nodded. She grabbed a chair next to mine.

"Lots of nice people have stopped by to offer their help in our time of need. But unfortunately, there isn't much we can do. The cruise-ship personnel are searching every corner of the ship, but it's like she has simply vanished." Mrs. Alessandrino inhaled sharply to stop herself from bursting into tears. I put my hand over hers. I felt a huge lump in my throat. I thought about my own daughter, Maya, and wanted badly to call her right now. I had seen her updates on Facebook and knew she was alright, but still. I wanted to hold her. Feel her in my arms. Make sure she was still here. Watching the sorrow in these people's eyes was unbearable.

"So, how much do you know thus far?" I asked.

Mrs. Alessandrino shook her head. "Not much. She was seen in the night-club downstairs and apparently left with some guy I've never seen before. The bartender was certain it was her when we reported her missing. Then, they pulled the surveillance photos and I...I simply can't understand how this can be my little girl. She would never do anything like this. It's just not her."

"And they're sure it was her?"

The woman sniffled and wiped her nose with a napkin. She got up from the chair and walked to a dresser.

"I have the pictures here. They gave us a copy. Would you believe they would serve drinks to a thirteen year-old? She's just a child."

Mrs. Alessandrino showed me the pictures and sat down again.

The girl certainly doesn't look thirteen in those pictures, I thought to myself. She was wearing a very tight dress and dancing wildly with a guy who, in several of the pictures, had his hands on her body.

"I really can't stand looking at those pictures," Mrs. Alessandrino sobbed. "I don't understand what is going on with her. It's like she's someone else all of a sudden."

"I know how you feel. I have a fourteen year-old myself and it felt like she changed overnight as well. Like, all of a sudden, she is this grown up who is nothing like the girl I used to know."

I flipped through the pictures from the club, then paused. "What is this?"

"That is a picture we had taken last night during dinner at the restaurant. The ship's photographer took it. It's the last picture we have of her... where she looks like herself and not this...this strange...," Mrs. Alessandrino paused. She wiped her eyes with the napkin, then sniffled. "It's the last time we were all together."

"You all look very happy."

"We were," Dr. Alessandrino suddenly said. "Who'd know that one stupid mistake could destroy such a beautiful picture? Could destroy our lives like this?"

"Now, Michael. We don't know if she is dead yet," Mrs. Alessandrino said. "She might just have slept in some cabin somewhere that they haven't searched yet. Remember, they told us that it will take them all day to go through the entire ship. Some of the people who have been out all night might still be sleeping. If she was that drunk, she might not wake up until later today. I still have my hopes up. Be the pessimist if you want, you old grumpy man. I refuse to believe the worst."

"I'm not believing anything. I know she is dead, woman. Don't you understand? I know she is gone," Dr. Alessandrino hissed.

"Don't listen to him. He always was the pessimistic one in our family," she said to me. "Not a good trait for a surgeon, right? I mean, if it was someone I loved who was going under the knife, I would like the doctor to be a little optimistic. But that was never my Michael. Not since...Well, not since he had a bad experience once. It's not something we talk about."

I nodded silently, not knowing what to say to all this. I wondered if it was a mistake to come. I had nothing to offer to these people in all their sorrow and worry. I held the Polaroid photo in my hand and looked at the family who appeared to be so happy. I wondered if they just pretended, just like we had tried to when the same photographer took our picture and everything went wrong. Was this entire trip just a mistake? Were we just pretending we were happy among each other?

"Are you alright, dear?" Mrs. Alessandrino asked.

"I'm fine. Sorry. I was just thinking of my own family. My daughter is not on this cruise with us. I just miss her all of a sudden."

"Take good care of her while you have her," Dr. Alessandrino said. "We tried everything to protect Francesca from the world, except for wrapping her in bubble-wrap. But it still wasn't enough. The one moment you're not paying attention can snap them away from you."

"Michael!" Mrs. Alessandrino hissed. "She's not dead yet."

"Yes, she is."

"No!" Mrs. Alessandrino was yelling with tears in her voice now. "No, she is not!"

"Then tell me where she is. Tell me."

"Arh, you old grumpy man," she snarled. "Just because of that old stupid story about those weird twins...Not everything in life has to end badly."

I got up from my chair. "I think I need to get back. But please let me know if there is anything I can do to help you in any way."

"That is awfully nice of you, dear," Mrs. Alessandrino said and followed me to the door. "I'm sure she'll turn up later today and then everything will be fine."

I listened to her say the words, but I could tell by the tone of her voice that she was losing confidence in them. She said them, but no longer believed them.

It broke my heart.

33

APRIL 1982

They came into the back of the truck in the morning, as usual. The twins were awake when the door opened and bright sunlight struck their faces. As usual, it was the two men who entered with sticks in their hands. And, as usual, they were supposed to beat up the twins as a part of their preparation ritual. They never fed them till nighttime, after the shows. Their breakfast always consisted of beating and humiliation.

The cage was opened and the two men stuck their hands in and grabbed the twins' arms. They pulled them out of the cage and threw them on the ground of the truck. The twins usually growled when someone touched them, but not this time. This time, they didn't make a sound as the men lifted their sticks and let them fall down hard on the twins' mutual body. They didn't moan in pain; they didn't snarl in anger.

They remained completely quiet.

"Freaks!" one of the men shouted.

The other one spat in their faces, then swung the stick and whipped them on their back till red stripes appeared on their bare skin.

Still, the twins made no sounds. They simply stared at the men, looking like they were waiting for something, waiting for the right moment.

It frightened the men. Everyone was afraid of the twins. Ever since the gang's fortune teller had made the prophecy. In her tea-leaves, she had seen the twins kill them all. Rip their bodies apart, one after another. That was why every gypsy in the gang wanted to beat them so badly. They wanted to beat the strength out of them, beat out the spite.

Sensing how the beating didn't affect the twins on this particular morning, the men became frustrated and increased the intensity. They made the strokes harder and wilder; they swung the sticks faster, and left very visible marks on their mutual body.

Still, there was no reaction.

"Monsters!" one of them yelled.

"Beasts!" the other one joined him. "Ugly, freaking beasts. Go back to hell where you came from."

The men were sweating, soaking their shirts under the arms and on the chest. They were frustrated now. The twins could see it in their eyes. They could smell it in their sweat. The sweet smell of anxiety.

"You two are the ugliest damn thing on this planet. Nasty drooling mutants," one of them continued.

He was circling the twins, while panting for air. Their back was striped from the beating. But they refused to feel any pain. Today was their birthday. At least, they had decided it was. This was the day when they would be re-born.

One of the men was looking at the other. "I don't know what's wrong with them today," he said.

"Mama Florea said to make them aggressive, so that's what we'll do," the other said. "We'll continue until they get angry."

"Fine by me," the first man said. He grabbed a baseball bat and lifted it in the air. With a huge roar, he ran towards the twins and swung it against them, when suddenly they reached up an arm and grabbed the bat in the air. With a strength that was barely human, they stopped it in mid-air.

The man gasped and let go. He watched with eyes wide open as they crushed the bat, splintered it into atoms in front of him, using nothing but one single hand.

For the first time since the men entered the truck, the twins showed some kind of emotion.

They smiled.

"What the hell...?" the other man said.

For years, the twins had hidden their true strength. They had taken the beatings because they thought they didn't deserve any better. They subdued themselves to others because they thought they weren't worth anything. They thought that, no matter where they went, people would only treat them the same way. But not anymore. On their twelfth birthday, the twins decided it was finally over.

They rose to their three feet like they had done in fighting the vicious dogs, opened their mouths and let out a growl that didn't sound human at all.

The men gasped and stumbled backwards, but before they knew it, the twins had fallen back to their arms and like a giant two-headed spider, and jumped both of them. With their long nails, they scratched their eyes out, then strangled them both simultaneously with their four bare hands.

34

APRIL 2014

The man didn't feel good. He was walking back and forth in his lower deck cabin sweating, rubbing his hands together, and trying hard to not lose control. It was so tough. So difficult for him to keep his thoughts from running off.

Something wasn't right. It wasn't good enough. He looked into the case where his creation lay. Deedee had gotten a new leg and extra skin to patch up where he needed it. But it wasn't good enough. The man had miscalculated somehow. The old skin was falling off fast now, like it was evaporating in front of his eyes. He didn't have enough. He had gotten rid of the girl's body in a hurry, once they started looking for her all over the ship. He had dissolved her with acid in the bathtub and made her disappear. He had scrubbed the floor clean of her blood, so no one would see it. Then, he had disinfected the entire cabin so none of her fingerprints would show up, in case they decided to examine his place.

But next thing he knew, Deedee was falling apart again. It wasn't going according to his plan. He needed to change his plans. Instead of going straight for the face, he realized he needed one more. He needed to act once again to have enough skin for the body. He only took what was on the back and abdomen because of the simple fact that it was the finest skin. And he only wanted the best and finest for Deedee. His skin was going to be soft and smooth as a baby's.

Yes, that was it. This time, he would cut off extra skin for later use.

"Stop walking around. You're making me sick," Deedee said. "What's the matter?"

"I don't think I feel so good, Deedee. I can't seem to...I can't...I feel like... I need to get more skin for you. It's...it's not enough."

"It's the fever," Deedee said. "You're burning up. It's making your brain mushy. You need to stay focused. Don't lose it. Don't lose control. I need you. Without you to help me, I'll die. You need to do something about that fever."

"I've tried, Deedee. I've tried everything. But it's just...It's like the pills aren't helping anything anymore. I've cleaned the wound, but the infection won't go away. The stitches are very painful. But they're worth it, Deedee. To have you close to me like this...I can't help it, Deedee. I really can't. I... I...Just feel so tired. I need...I don't know what I need. I need to focus... that's what I need. Yes. Yes. Focus. Stay on the path."

"You're losing it," Deedee said.

"NO!" the man yelled.

Deedee went silent. The man regretted his outburst. "I'm sorry, Deedee. I'm sorry for yelling at you. It's just...I'm fine. You don't have to worry about me. You hear me? Don't worry about me."

"As you say. I'll try not to."

"You have plenty of worries of your own," the man said, trying hard to sound convincing. "It's all about you, remember? I'm doing all of this for you. Don't you ever forget that."

"I know."

"Good. Then we're all good. I'll get you one more donor. Maybe I'll get you a new arm this time, huh? I think you could use that. And then patch you up where it's needed." The man smiled, trying hard to not let Deedee know just how bad a condition he really was in. There was no need for him to know that. He would only be saddened. The man really didn't want him to be. He wanted him to be happy. Like in the song they played constantly now. *Happy. Happy. Happy. Because I'm happy. Happy. Happy. Happy.*

Yes, the man wanted Deedee to smile and...laugh. He wanted him to laugh with happiness.

"I would like that," Deedee said. "I would really like that."

The man burst into a manic laughter. He shook his head to try and get rid of the tic in his right eye. "Splendid. That's settled then. I'll get it to you right away. First, we have a delivery to make."

The man put on his black coat and covered Deedee up underneath, while whispering:

"See you later."

35

APRIL 2014

Victor hadn't moved an inch when I got back to the suite. He didn't even look at me when I came through the door. Christoffer was in his room.

"Hi buddy. I'm back," I said and sat on the couch next to him.

A new program had started on TV. It was another one of those about deformed children born all over the world. He seemed to be all into it. I exhaled and tried to watch some of it, but found it hard to look at all these misshapen children...some with four arms, other with huge lumps growing out of their heads. They even showed pictures of an Indian man who had lived all of his life with his twin inside of his body. Now, it was time for it to be removed by the doctors.

I felt slightly nauseated. I looked at Victor instead. How badly I wanted to hold him in my arms and stay like that. I kept thinking about Mr. and Mrs. Alessandrino and the look I had seen in their eyes. The look of despair. The look of hopelessness. Losing your child had to be the worst thing in the world. I was so lucky to still have both of mine. Even if our circumstances weren't perfect.

I grabbed my phone and found Maya's number. I looked at it for a while, biting my lip. Should I call her? I desperately wanted to. But I was also afraid of smothering her. Of pushing her further away by not giving her the space she needed. She was doing well, according to her posts on Facebook. I had nothing to worry about.

But I miss her so much. It's eating me up. Just one call? Just one quick 'hi are you alright, I miss you,' call? That can't be so bad can it?

I exhaled and put the phone down again. No. I had to be strong. She wasn't going to pick up anyway. I would just end up leaving one of those silly embarrassing messages that would make her roll her eyes at me.

Oh my God. I even miss her eye-rolling.

I walked out on the balcony where the sun was still strong in the clear blue sky. I closed my eyes and let it warm me up. I had missed the sun. Winters in Denmark were brutal. It felt like months since I had last seen the light from the sun. It was so bright, so life-giving.

I sat in a chair and enjoyed it for a little while. Thoughts flickered quickly through my mind. It hurt me to think about those parents in the suite not far from mine who were still waiting to hear news about their daughter, while we moved further and further away from where she could possibly have fallen in the water. It was cruel.

I kept returning to the Colombo family. Victor told me she had killed herself because she couldn't bear to go on without her son. I found it to be a very drastic and slightly unlikely explanation. I mean, at least wait till you get some answers, wait till you're certain he is really dead.

I didn't understand it. It made no sense. Victor had told me Mrs. Colombo had *known* that her son was dead. He had repeated it twice. I didn't understand how she could have known it. I mean, there was always hope, wasn't there? Did she just conclude it like Mr. Alessandrino? Just because she had a pessimistic nature? Was a hunch really enough for someone to kill herself? Even in Mr. Alessandrino, there had to be some hope, right?

I opened my eyes and looked out at the moving ocean. I kept imagining the girl falling from the railing. Would the fall kill her? Maybe not, but she would probably drown, right? The water was warm, though. Maybe if she was a good swimmer? If a boat picked her up?

I shook my head. No. It had happened in the middle of the night. In this darkness, she would be more than lucky if a boat was able to find her. It wasn't very realistic.

I turned to walk back to Victor, when suddenly a loud scream resounded through the walls of the ship.

36

APRIL 2014

I stormed into the hallway, carefully closing the door till it locked behind me, so no one could get to Victor or Christoffer.

The screams came from further down the hallway. I ran towards the sound and stopped at Mr. and Mrs. Alessandrino's door. It was ajar and Mrs. Alessandrino was kneeling on the floor while screaming. She was holding something in her hand. A photo.

"Mrs. Alessandrino," I said and came closer to her. Mr. Alessandrino was standing behind her, not uttering a word, but with a look of terror on his face.

"What's wrong?" I asked.

The woman stopped screaming, she threw the photo on the floor and threw herself into the arms of her husband. He seemed to be in shock and hardly moved. He didn't even put his arm around her. She sobbed and screamed into his shirt.

I picked up the photo and looked at it. Then I gasped. "What is this?"

"It's her," Mr. Alessandrino said, emotionless. "It's a picture of Francesca's chopped off leg. It was pushed under our door a few minutes ago. When we opened the door, no one was there."

I felt sick to my stomach. I stared at the picture. The leg was smeared in blood. A cut off bone stuck out on the top where it had been sawed off. "...but? ...Are...are you sure that it is her?"

"Positive," Mr. Alessandrino said. He was staring right through me. His look was empty. "Look at the scar on her knee. She got that from falling from a tree when she was eight. Eight stitches. I took her to the hospital myself."

A lump of tears grew in my throat. I had no idea what to say. Mrs. Alessandrino was crying hysterically. People had gathered outside the suite. I could hear their voices asking what was going on.

"Emma?" one of the voices said. I felt a hand on my shoulder. I looked up and saw my dad. "She's dead," I whispered with a shivering voice. "Someone killed their daughter." I showed him the picture.

"Oh my God," my dad exclaimed.

He closed the door behind us, telling people to go back to their suites and leave the family to their grief. I grabbed Mrs. Alessandrino and helped her to lie down on a couch. My dad helped Mr. Alessandrino to sit down.

"I'll call for the ship's doctor," I said, and grabbed the suite's phone on the wall. I dialed zero to reach the receptionist and told her we needed the doctor immediately. A few minutes later, he knocked on the door. I opened it and let him in.

"What's going on?" he asked. His gentle eyes smiled compassionately.

I explained what had happened. "I think they might both need a sedative. I don't want either of them to do something they'll regret later, if you understand," I said, thinking of Mrs. Colombo and her possible suicide. "And then, I think it's time to call the police."

The doctor nodded. "I'll take care of it."

"Good."

I held Mrs. Alessandrino's hand while the doctor sedated her. I couldn't stand the look in her eyes. Such misery. Such anguish. "I have to get back to my son and his friend now. Let me know if there is anything I can do for you," I said.

Mrs. Alessandrino shook her head slowly. I could tell the sedative was already kicking in. Her eyes went numb and the gloom lightened, as she slowly drifted away. I felt my dad's hand in mine.

"Let's leave them to their grief," he said.

I nodded. It was the right thing to do. We could check in on them later.

I placed the photograph on the table for the police to find. I was starting to look forward to getting off this ship. Once the police were notified about the murder, they would definitely order the captain to find the nearest harbor. I was hoping it wouldn't take too long. I wanted to leave, to feel solid ground underneath my feet again. I didn't feel safe on this ship with a murderer on the loose.

37

APRIL 2014

M y dad went back to my suite with me. I was shaking all over.

"This is terrible, Dad," I said, and opened the door.

Victor didn't look away from his TV. Christoffer was lying on the bed in his room, reading.

"I mean, those poor parents."

I grabbed two beers and some chocolate from the mini-bar and handed it to my dad. We sat on the couch next to Victor and drank in silence. I felt horrible. My dad put his arm around my shoulder.

"This trip was a mistake," he said. "It was a disaster waiting to happen. I never should have bought the tickets."

"Don't say that. It isn't your fault. You did everything you could. You ordered the best suites and treated us like royalty. It's not your fault all this happened."

"It's not just the killings. I mean, that is terrifying, don't get me wrong, but I guess I should have known better concerning you and your mother. I should have known it was too early for you. I know you're still angry with her for leaving, but...," my dad paused and drank.

"But what, dad?"

"I just thought that, if I'm able to forgive her, then you should be too."

I rubbed my forehead. A headache was starting. "I know. You're right. It's not that I don't forgive her, it's just that I don't feel like she is really trying hard enough."

My dad gave me a look.

"Okay, you're right again," I said. "I do find it hard to forgive her for what she did to you and me. She wasn't even there when I went through the divorce and finding out that Michael was cheating on me. Then there was all the stuff going on with Victor and running to all the doctors. I could really have used a mother back then."

"You had your dad."

"I did. And you were great. I couldn't have done it without you, thank you. But a mother would have been nice to have as well. Now, it's like she doesn't understand anything."

"Well, do you really think she would have gotten it back then?"

"What do you mean?"

"You know how your mother is. How do you think she would have reacted to the fact that Michael was cheating on you?"

I ate a piece of chocolate, while realizing how right he was. "She would probably have told me I hadn't done enough to hold on to him."

"Exactly. And to all of Victor's problems? What would she have said to that?"

"That I hadn't disciplined him enough. Oh my God, Dad, you're so right. It wouldn't have been any different. As a matter of fact, she would only have made my life even more miserable than it already was. I had this picture of her comforting me and taking care of me, but that's not how she is."

"I love your mom, but when it comes to her daughter, it's somehow never good enough. Nothing you do is good enough for her. It's not one of my favorite traits of hers, but I can live with it," he said with a light chuckle. "You have to understand where she's coming from. Your mom thinks criticizing you helps you. She thinks it will toughen you up. That's the way she was brought up herself, so she sees nothing wrong with it. I know for a fact that she is very proud of you and all you have accomplished. She just never tells you that."

I stared at him in surprise. "Guess I should be careful to not make the same mistake with my daughter too then, huh?" I said and ate the last piece of chocolate.

"That sounds like a plan."

I looked at the TV screen where the documentary was still running. Now it was showing pictures of a pair of conjoined twins from Rome that, for years, had lived in and terrorized the streets of the city back in the eighties. Many people thought they were a beast escaped from hell and feared to meet them, since the rumors said it meant certain death.

I looked at the pictures from back then. A bad photograph, taken by tourists, showed them in an alley going through a dumpster behind a restaurant.

I shook my head, thinking people were stupid with all their superstition. Then I paused.

"What's wrong?" my dad asked.

"Photograph," I mumbled.

"What about it?"

"Mrs. Alessandrino received a photo of her daughter's cut off leg. Mrs. Colombo was certain her son was dead. Why was she so sure that she would kill herself?"

"You think she received a photo as well?"

I put the empty beer bottle down. "I need to check something. Could you stay here with the boys?"

"No problem."

38

APRIL 1984

At fourteen years of age, the twins were terrorizing the streets of Rome. At least, according to the citizens.

Before running into the streets, they had killed them all. Just like in the fortune teller's prophecy, the twins had killed every gypsy in the gang that morning in the parking lot. Like a mighty spider, they had jumped the roofs of the trucks, swung themselves inside the open windows and massacred the men and women who had tortured them and kept them locked up for years.

Then, they had disappeared into the streets. They lived in the dark alleys, staying clear of people, and eating trash out of the dumpsters behind the restaurants. Soon, rumors started running about the beast from hell, the two-headed spider mutant that was rampaging the small streets of Rome. Some said it was a large animal, others said it was a vampire or a mutant rat. It was even said to maybe be a mythical creature, like a sphinx with the body of a lion and a human head, or a Scorpion man, half scorpion, half man. No matter what kind of creature it was, most stuck with the theory that it was very dangerous and came from the pit of hell.

The newspapers even wrote about the mystical creature that had been seen by people in the streets and soon, tourists roamed the alleys in the hope of catching a glimpse of the strange creature and maybe even taking a photo.

But the twins hid well and were hardly ever seen. They didn't care much about people, only to stay as far away from them as possible. They slept in abandoned buildings and ate what they could get their hands on. Whether it was leftovers from the restaurants left in the dumpster or a small cat that they killed themselves, didn't matter to them. It was all down to survival and not getting caught or seen by people.

They had started speaking again in their own language and would have long conversations at nighttime. They would often speak of their parents that they had never known and make up stories about them and where they were. They would imagine their parents looking for them everywhere, not knowing where to find them. They would talk about how their dad probably was a pilot or something really important, how they might have been stolen as children and, ever since, their parents had been searching everywhere to find them.

They knew, of course, this wasn't true, but it helped them to get over the fact that they both knew why they had no parents. Because no one wanted them, because who would ever want the spider-boys? Who would want a beast for child? They both knew that was why they had been abandoned, but it felt good to escape into their little fantasy every now and then.

And it helped that they had each other. Without their mutual love for one another, they wouldn't have survived any of what they had gone though. They both knew that and never stopped telling each other how important the other one was.

Every night, they crawled onto the dirty old mattress they had found in an old condemned building, looked at each other and spoke the words:

"I love you."

"I love you more."

And so they did as well on this night, precisely two years after the attack on the gypsies. The night of what they had decided was their birthday. They had just eaten the remains of a stray dog they had captured near the famous Piazza Navona and told each other goodnight, when a shadow entered the room, followed by several others.

It was a sound that woke them up. The twins opened their eyes, a flash-light was turned on and the twins could see faces behind it. One was holding a tranquillizer-gun that he had pointed at them. The twins barely managed to scream before the shot was fired.

39

APRIL 2014

I walked down the hallway and came to the door to room three hundred and forty five. The numbers had been imprinted in my mind ever since Victor had said them over and over again. I touched the handle carefully and realized the door wasn't locked. I opened it and went under the police tape.

There was still blood on the beige carpet in the bedroom where Ivana Colombo had been shot. I took in a deep breath to calm myself down. The thought of all the despair and suffering that had taken place in this room made me miserable. I had to pull myself together in order to focus on why I was there.

I walked to the stain on the floor and looked around. The police had been in the room for hours, examining the entire suite. If I was to find something they hadn't, it had to be hidden pretty well.

I tried to imagine I was Ivana Colombo and sat on the bed. I imagined that someone stuck a photograph under the door, then maybe knocked to get their attention. Ivana would get up from the bed and walk towards the door and open it. I got up and tried to do the same. I pretended to open the door, then looked down and imagined a photograph on the floor. I visualized Ivana picking it up, then the shock.

What did she do next? Did she turn to her husband and show him the picture? No, she couldn't have. Then he would have told that to the police and that would have supported his testimony that it was suicide. So maybe she didn't tell him. Maybe the shock was so strong, all she could think of was to kill herself. Find the gun and finish it off. Shut up the strong emotion of grief that was about to rush in over her.

I looked around, then walked back to the bedroom. The shot was fired in there. So she had to have walked back in there to grab the gun. I walked back, pretending to be holding the photograph.

She had to have been really out of it at this point. Maybe walking back and forth in the room deciding what to do? Or was she determined it was the only way out from the moment she saw the photo? After all, she had to have thought it through while waiting for answers. Maybe she even planned it. Maybe she decided it already once he went missing, that if Alberto turned up dead, she would shoot herself right away...Determined that there was no way she was ever going to go on without him.

But where was the gun? I opened the drawer next to the bed, but found only a Bible and some pens with the cruise line's logo on them. I closed the drawer, went to the other side of the bed and opened that one as well. The gun had to have some case or something, right? I didn't know much about guns, I had to admit. I had never even held one in my hands. Where I came from, we were very much against weapons. I had no idea why a woman like Ivana Colombo would have a gun with her in the first place. Was it because she was afraid of being attacked? Maybe, being this rich, she was constantly afraid of having her child kidnapped for ransom, or just someone assaulting them to get their money and valuables. Did she bring expensive jewelry with her on a trip like this? Probably. To wear at nice dinners and such. Now, wouldn't you try and have the gun near the jewelry, in case someone forced an entry?

I walked to the dresser and opened all the drawers. I only found clothes. Expensive underwear. I felt bad for going through her stuff and closed all the drawers again.

"Now, where would you hide jewelry and a gun, Mrs. Colombo?" I mumbled.

Then I realized the obvious. There was a safe. In every suite, there was a small safe for the guests to put their valuables in. Just like in many hotels. I found it in the walk-in closet. On a shelf above the hangers. It was locked. I took out my phone and searched the web for *how to open a hotel safe,* then typed the brand of it. I found a video on YouTube telling me to type in only zeroes. The man in the video told me most of these kinds of safes from this manufacturer had the same defect. You could open all of them by simply using zeroes. So I did. I typed them in and the safe opened.

I was quite startled that it was this easy. I opened it and looked inside. As I suspected, I found jewelry and a black case for the gun. The case was empty. Carefully placed next to it was a Polaroid photograph.

"Bingo," I said and picked it up. I felt nauseated again. The picture showed Alberto Colombo, lying on his back with dead empty eyes. His chest and stomach had been flayed.

Ivana Colombo had placed it there as the last thing before taking the gun, probably thinking they would find it there and understand why she killed herself. It was her suicide note to the world. She just never considered the possibility that they might not find it...simply because they weren't looking.

40

APRIL 2014

The man was watching the people by the pool. So many happy faces. So much laughter. It annoyed him. Especially since he himself didn't feel well. He was aching all over, shaking, and burning up with fever. The damn wound on his shoulder hurt again. He had taken pills to kill it, but it didn't seem to be enough.

He had put Deedee back in his case to not attract attention. A man in a long black coat is, after all, quite suspicious on the sundeck where most people were wearing swimsuits. But now, the wounds from where Deedee had been were bleeding and he could see red spots through the white shirt of his uniform. He put on a jacket to cover it up. It hurt like crazy.

Just a few hours more, then everything will be perfected. You just need to stay focused a little longer, just enough to finish the work you started. You can't give up now. Do it for Deedee.

It didn't take long for the man to spot a new donor. A young boy playing in the water. His skin was perfect. The man didn't have to come close to be able to judge that. He was perfect. And being slightly chubby, especially on the stomach, he would provide skin enough. A lot of the finest skin.

The man hadn't had enough time to plan his approach well, and he knew he was taking a chance. But, as soon as the mother told the boy to get out of the water because they had to get something to eat, the man followed them closely back to their cabin on the middle deck. The boy wasn't among the rich people on the boat, which the man usually preferred, since they took better care of their skin, but he would have to do. There wasn't time to change plans now.

The mother and child disappeared into the cabin, then returned a few minutes later all dressed. The man followed them as they walked into a fast-food restaurant and ordered fried chicken and French fries. The man frowned while watching them throw themselves at the greasy food. None of what they ate could be good for their skin. He had started to regret his choice. Then he looked around him to see if someone else would be better. He spotted another boy walking into a toy store with his mother and wondered if he would be a better choice. He followed them with his eyes as they disappeared into the store next to the fast-food restaurant.

The man shook his head. No. No. He had made his choice. He had to follow through with it. He looked at the chubby boy again. He was licking grease off his fingers, then washing the food down with soda.

No, it doesn't matter. You need him. Take him.

The man waited till the boy had to go to the restroom, then followed him in there. The boy was standing by the urinals and was peeing when the man came up to him. The chubby boy looked at him, annoyed.

"Hey, do you mind? I don't like people staring at me while I'm peeing," the boy said.

The man tilted his head and came closer.

"Hey, didn't you hear me?" the boy said. "Find someone else's penis to stare at before I call the police."

The man didn't move. He felt the handle of the knife in his pocket. Then a thought struck him.

How will you carry him downstairs without anyone noticing?

He hadn't thought it through. It was so hard for him to think straight lately. It was like the fever made it impossible. He was breathing heavily, while staring at the boy. Then a dizziness overpowered him and he had to lean on the wall to not fall.

The boy stared at him in disgust. Then he closed his zipper and started walking towards the door. The man held on to the wall while fighting to stay conscious. Slowly, he slid towards the floor till his face landed on the cold tiles. The boy turned to look at him. Then he walked up to him and kicked him in the abdomen, knocking out the last bit of air he had left.

"Old pig," the boy said, just as he walked through the door and returned to the restaurant.

41

APRIL 2014

I still had the photograph in my hand as I ran to my own suite. My dad had dozed off on the couch next to Victor when I stormed inside.

"She killed herself," I said.

My dad squinted. "I'm not sure I'm following you here," he said drowsily.

"Victor was right. Victor knew, Dad. He told me Mrs. Colombo knew her son was dead and that was why she shot herself. It wasn't the husband at all."

"Victor told you this?" my dad asked.

"Yes. And I have the proof," I said and handed him the photograph. "I found it in the safe next to the empty gun case. She put it there as the last thing she did. That's how she knew. That's how she knew her son was dead. The killer slipped the photo underneath the door like he did to Mr. and Mrs. Alessandrino. The police just never found the photo because she placed it in the safe and, apparently, they never looked in there."

"Wow, Emma," my dad said. "That's a lot to take in at once. So, you're saying Mr. Colombo never killed anyone?"

"Exactly. I just need to get the proof to the police. I'm expecting the captain to let us know that he will find the nearest harbor any minute now. The police need to take over."

I sat down next to Victor. He looked at me all of a sudden, then at the photo in my hand. He was fascinated by it, I could tell. I hated that he liked stuff like this, but it was different with him, I kept reminding myself. He didn't react to things like the rest of us. He didn't find them appalling or disgusting. He found the macabre interesting, in a scientific way. I was starting to think he might have a future in forensics.

"You were right, buddy," I said.

I stared at the photo and started wondering about it. Who was it that had placed it under the door? Who was this strange killer on the ship? He was using a Polaroid camera. Not many did that anymore.

I turned to look at my dad. "Mr. and Mrs. Alessandrino had their picture taken with their daughter on the evening before she disappeared. I saw it in their room."

"Yeah. So what?" my dad asked with a yawn. "Lots of people get their photo taken on board."

"Yeah, but think of it. It's a Polaroid photo. They're pretty rare these days. Both pictures taken of the victims were taken with Polaroid cameras as well."

"So, you think it's the photographer? He's working for the cruise line, you know. He's not some random guy taking pictures of people. It's his living. He uses Polaroid because people like the fact that they get the picture right away as a souvenir. I spoke to him the other day and he is a very interesting man. He likes to do the old-school instant photos for people and considers it an art-form in a world where everyone else relies on automatic digital cameras. We had a very interesting talk about it. He's been everywhere. He's been a fixture at festivals, parades and concerts, selling instant portraits to locals and tourists for many years."

"Okay. But just think of it for a second. It's a perfect way to find victims, right? I mean he gets close to everyone onboard. He gets to check them out and choose who he wants to attack," I said pensively.

My dad looked at me like I had lost it. "That's a little far-fetched Emma."

"Oh my God," I said. "He took our picture as well. Do you think he was checking us out too?"

My dad snorted. "I don't know. I don't think it's very clever of us to walk around accusing people like this. At least be careful."

"I will. I'll tell the police my theory once they get here. It can't be long now before something happens. The entire ship must know about the photo by now. They must have called for the police."

As I spoke, someone knocked on my door. I went to open it. My mom burst in. Her cheeks were red. She was carrying several shopping bags.

"Oh my God. You won't believe the deals I've made today. Now, I know I've spent a little too much, Bengt, but bear with me. I have bought the most amazing stuff. Most of it is, after all, *for your eyes only*."

She paused and looked at us. "My, oh my. Why the gloomy faces?"

My dad got up and walked to her. "Don't freak out, Ulla. But we believe there is a killer on the loose on the ship. He killed both Alberto Colombo and Francesca Alessandrino. Maybe he even also killed the guy that Francesca was seen with. Emma thinks he might have had his eyes on us too."

"Oh, my God," my mother burst out.

"What?"

"There was a lot of turmoil downstairs on the shopping and dining deck. I talked to this woman and she told me there was a guy in the bathroom who had fainted. They found him lying on the floor, bleeding from his shoulder. Do you think someone tried to kill him?"

I looked at my dad. "I don't know," I said. "I think I'll go and check it out. If the police have arrived, I want to talk to them. Could you two watch Victor and Christoffer for me?"

"Of course," my dad said.

My mother grabbed my arm when I passed her. She pulled me close and kissed my forehead.

"Be careful, sweetheart."

I smiled at her. She did know how to be a mother after all.

42

APRIL 1984

T he twins woke up in a different kind of cage. A small closed room with no windows and only white walls. They were lying on a bed, but could hardly move. They had been strapped down. All four arms and three legs were tied to the bed and, no matter how much they pulled and moved around, they stayed that way.

They turned their heads and looked into each other's eyes, both of them sensing the other's deep fear. Many things had happened to them in their short time on this earth. But never this.

They had no idea where they were or who was holding them captive, but they were determined to get out. They had tried to live a life of freedom and they weren't going to let go of that at any cost.

They waited for many hours before the door to the room finally opened and someone entered. A group of four men in white coats, with charts in their hands and serious faces.

"We had to strap them down," the man in the front wearing glasses said, as the others followed him inside. "We were afraid they might hurt someone or themselves."

The twins gasped, then tried to break loose by pulling forcefully on the straps, but nothing happened. The twins growled and snarled as the group came closer. Never had the twins seen anything like these people and, given their past with people, they immediately feared the worst from them.

The men spoke amongst each other, while looking at the twins from all directions and angles. They walked around the bed and stared at them, then made notes on their pads and charts, while nodding and agreeing. The first man spoke and said things the twins didn't understand. Sentences including words like *Mental and Behavioral disorder* filled the room and the twins had no idea what they meant or how it would affect their future. But they knew it wasn't good. These men didn't want them for anything good.

They howled and barked if the men came too close. They snapped their teeth at them to have them keep their distance.

"We had to cut their nails so they wouldn't scratch any of the personnel here or themselves," the man with the glasses continued.

"It's truly extraordinary," another man said and scratched his beard. "Don't think I have ever seen anything like this before."

The men agreed and mumbled between themselves. The twins cringed in fear, as the eyes in the room kept examining them and their mutual body. One of the men lifted an arm carefully to look at the twin's abdomen. The twins snapped their teeth at him. He gasped and pulled backwards.

"As you gentlemen might see, we do believe there is no future for them in our society if they stay conjoined," the one with glasses continued. "We do believe it would serve both of them best if they were separated. That's the only way we can start treatment of them separately. The way it is now, they seem to only be interested in each other and nothing else. They even speak their own language between them that no one else understands."

"I concur," another of the men said. "The only way these two can get better and get a life is if they're separated."

"But, you really think it's possible?" another one said. "I mean, they share lots of vital organs, don't they? A surgery like this is usually best done at birth, am I correct?"

The man with the glasses nodded, then pulled out a big picture and showed it to them. "As our examination of them while they were sedated shows, they each have their own brain, heart and two kidneys; they only have one liver and a single reproductive organ. Their third leg is vestigial and the twins keep it concealed in their clothing. They can stand, but they cannot walk; they crawl on their hands and feet, which is why they have long been known as the *Spider-boys*. The twins are joined at the abdomen and pelvis, have four arms, and three legs. So, if you look at it, all they really share is the liver and their reproductive organ. The way I see it, separation is not only possible, it's a must. Their body won't be able to continue to sustain keeping both of them alive. Just the fact that they're walking on their arms provides an unnecessary strain on their joints. It's just not natural what they're doing. Not to mention their psychological state of mind. The way it is now, they're like wild animals. No one has taken care of them and they need our help. Now, after the surgery the one on the left will have two legs, the other only one, and will not be able to walk. But the way I see it, at least one of them will have the chance to have a completely normal life. The other will be in a wheelchair for the rest of his life, but will still be able to live close to normally. Time will tell if a liver transplant is needed. With the right medicine and behavioral therapy afterwards, I believe we can make it far with them. I will, of course, perform the procedure myself."

The bearded man patted the man with the glasses on the shoulder. "Surgery to separate conjoined twins is an extremely complex surgery, depending of course on the point of attachment and the internal parts that are shared. Most cases of separation are extremely risky and life-threatening. If you pull this off, your name will be in the books of medical history my friend. You'll be up there with Dr. Bertram Katz, who performed the first separation in 1957."

The man with the glasses nodded. He smiled with satisfaction while his colleague spoke.

"Dr. Alessandrino, the world-renowned surgeon who was first to successfully separate teen-aged conjoined twins. That is truly something, huh?"

Then they all left, nodding and mumbling.

Back in the room, the twins had become quiet as the grave. They might not be able to understand many things, but they knew what *separation* meant.

43

APRIL 2014

The man saw a bright light and thought for a second he might have died. Until he opened his eyes and realized the light was coming from the lamp above his head, the lamp lighting up the dark restroom on the ship.

His shoulder was hurting badly and he groaned while trying to get up. A voice reached him from beyond the bright light.

"Are you alright, sir?"

The man squinted. He spotted a dark face in the distance. "What... what happened?" he asked.

"I believe you fainted, sir."

The man blinked his eyes several times and now realized a crowd had gathered in the restroom and they were all looking at him.

"Are you alright, sir?" someone repeated.

The man grunted. He sat up and held a hand to his hurting shoulder, while everything slowly came back to him. The failed attempt to catch another donor, the dizziness, the sea of stars that he had plunged into as the boy had left calling him an old pig.

"I'm fine," he growled.

He tried to get up. Someone grabbed his arm and helped him.

"I think you're bleeding, sir. Do you want me to call for help?"

The man shook his head. He needed to get away before the boy said anything to his mother. He had no idea how long he had been lying on the floor.

"Deedee," he mumbled and let himself be pulled up from the ground.

"What was that?"

The man shook his head. He felt drops of sweat roll across his forehead. His cheeks were burning. He had to get ahold of some penicillin.

"Nothing. I just...I just need to...If I could only...," he pointed at the door and the crowd spread and let him exit the restroom. The man hurried through the fast-food restaurant and spotted the boy sitting next to his mother playing his Gameboy. The man breathed a sigh of relief. He hadn't said anything.

The man staggered through the ship's corridors, while he sensed how he was slowly regaining his strength and ability to think straight.

Deedee needs you. Deedee needs a donor. Can't give up now. Not when we're this close. You need to focus on what's important now.

The man didn't have to think for long before he knew what to do. He had messed up. The boy in the restroom had seen his face and would tell as soon as another boy disappeared. He would tell them about the strange man in the restroom. Then they would know who to look for. They would come for him. The man couldn't risk being stopped. Not now that he was so close. He had to move on with his plan. Before anyone was on to him. This was more important than anything else.

The man stormed up the stairs to the upper deck, then paused to catch his breath. He walked slowly towards the room where he knew the boy was staying. The man had kept a close eye on him ever since he saw him on the deck on the day of the departure.

As the man was walking towards the door, it opened and he decided to continue straight ahead. The woman the man believed was the boy's mother exited looking very determined and closed the door behind her. The man smiled at her and nodded politely as he walked past her room. The woman smiled back, said a quiet "Hello," then continued in the opposite direction.

I can't believe our luck, Deedee. Did you see it, did you? She didn't bring the boy. She left him in the room, Deedee. I can't believe it. Soon you'll have your face. I promise it.

The man pulled out a card and put it in the reader. He slid it soundlessly and waited for the click-sound and the green lamp to flash.

Then, he entered. The younger boy was lying on the couch in the living room of the suite. The other was in the smaller bedroom, also asleep. The man approached him walking silently across the carpets. Then he stopped. There was a sound from somewhere else. It sounded like it came from the master bedroom. The door was closed. The man held his breath. Was there someone in there? Who?

The man shook his head. It didn't matter. The people in there seemed busy. A woman whined in joy. The man concentrated on the boy. He snuck closer. The boy's eyes were closed. His breathing calm. He seemed to be asleep.

Just a few minutes more, Deedee. Just a little longer.

The man reached into his pocket and pulled out a syringe. Without making a sound, he placed it on the boy's bare thigh, right where the shorts stopped and pressed it through the skin with a small groan of pleasure.

Now he's ours Deedee. He's all ours.

44

APRIL 2014

I went downstairs and walked around a little. My mom told me the man had fainted in the bathroom next to the fried chicken place. I walked in there and close to the men's bathroom, but no one was there. There wasn't even a crowd of people. I asked a guy coming out of the restroom and he told me he hadn't seen or heard anything.

I decided it had to be another restroom, so I started going through all of them on the deck. But I found no man that had fainted or anyone who could tell me about it. I stopped several strangers on my way and asked if they knew about a guy fainting in the bathroom, but no one could tell me anything.

It was all a little odd, I thought.

After about twenty minutes, I decided to get back. I wasn't getting anywhere with this. Maybe him fainting had nothing to do with the killings. After all, he could just have been sick or something.

Except your mom said he was bleeding from the shoulder.

Well, he could have hurt himself, right? Maybe he fainted and hurt his shoulder in the fall. I took the ship's elevator back to my deck, then walked to my suite's door and slid my card through the reader. I opened it and walked inside. I noticed the ship was hardly moving anymore and, suddenly, it came to a stop. I was surprised by this, since I had expected it to find harbor as soon as possible.

"Mom? Dad? I'm back. I couldn't..."

I froze immediately. There was no one here? "Mom? Dad? Victor?" I asked.

I walked into the living room and found Victor sleeping on the couch. The TV was still on, but where were my mom and dad? Where was Christoffer? I turned off the TV, walked to his room, and found it empty. That was strange. Had they gone back to their suite and taken only Christoffer with them?

"Mom? Dad?" I asked again.

Then I heard it. The sound no child should ever have to hear. The sound of my parents having sex.

Oh, my God! Oh my...they're doing it in my bedroom?!

I had no idea what to do with myself. I felt infuriated and embarrassed, all at the same time. But most of all, I felt frustrated because I had no idea where Christoffer was. And what about Victor? Had he heard any of this?

How can they be this irresponsible? They're supposed to be grown-ups. They're my parents, for crying out loud.

I had no idea what to do next. I was standing there, listening to my mother whine and my dad groan, covering my ears with my hands.

This is crazy! What do I do? I can't go in there. I simply can't. I don't want to see them like this. But I need to know where Christoffer is. And I need this to stop. I need to let them know I'm in here. Let them know that I can HEAR them!

I felt mostly like screaming. So, that's what I did. I yelled their names. Standing right outside their door.

"ULLA and BENGT!"

The noise stopped. I looked at Victor. He moved, but was still sleeping. There was turmoil behind the door and I moved away. I heard fumbling, chitchatting, and someone moving fast. Finally, my dad came out. His thin hair was messy and his clothes were disorganized. He was blushing and panting at the same time.

"Emma! You're back," he said.

"Yes. Yes, I am," I said, talking way too loud and shrill.

"Well, your mom and I were just...," he straightened his hair back while he searched for an explanation. It was painful to both watch and hear. "Well, we were just...taking a little nap."

"Don't even try," I said.

My dad chuckled. "Sorry. Guess you heard us?"

"Kind of hard not to."

"Sorry about that."

I exhaled. My dad had a blissful look on his face. I was thrilled to see him this happy, I had to admit. Even given the circumstances. I just wished it hadn't been in my bed. I would have to have one of the maids come to my room and change the sheets.

"Just don't do it in my bed again, alright?"

My mom came out of the bedroom. She was blushing as well. "Emma? Is that you? You're back fast."

I shook my head, trying to erase the mental images I had made. I really wanted to forget it.

"Let's not talk about it anymore," I said. "Where is Christoffer?"

My mom and dad looked at each other then at the couch in the living room where Victor was sleeping. My mom walked to Christoffer's bedroom.

"He's not here?" my dad asked.

My heart started racing in my chest. "You mean to tell me you don't know where Christoffer is?"

"Easy now, Emma," my mother said. "He's must be here somewhere. Maybe he is hiding...Have you checked everywhere?"

I stormed back into the living room, calling his name.

"Christoffer?"

With angry and frustrated steps, I walked onto the balcony and looked for him, then the bathroom, and the bedroom, checking the closet, underneath the bed and any place he could be hiding.

"I don't understand this, Emma," my dad said. "I swear he was in his room. Sound asleep. We would never have gone in the bedroom if he was awake. They were both asleep, so we thought there wouldn't be any harm in..."

"It's the truth, Emma. They were both asleep when your dad and I decided to...," she looked at my father. Then she looked down. "To also take a little nap."

"I can't believe this," I growled at them, infuriated. "I left you in charge of the boys and now one of them is gone. What the hell were you thinking?"

Victor woke up now. He sat up and rubbed his eyes.

"Now, easy there, Emma," my dad said. "Your mother is right. He fell asleep on the bed. Let's think about this for a little while. I mean, what can have happened here? No one can get in here when the door is locked. He must be hiding here somewhere. I...I...can't see how..."

"Of course you can't. But that's what happened. He is missing. Just like the Alberto Colombo kid and Francesca Alessandrino. All because you didn't keep an eye on him like I told you to. All because you couldn't...keep your hands to yourselves."

45

APRIL 2014

I was so angry I couldn't stand still. My mom and dad looked like children who had messed up. They were coming up with new excuses and trying to calm me down.

"Now Emma, let's try and be reasonable here," my dad said. "We need to think this through first, alright?"

"Yes," my mom said. "We can't jump to any conclusions now. We need to keep our heads clear."

It didn't work. I stared, infuriated, at my irresponsible parents while a thousand thoughts flickered through my mind. Where could he be? Had the killer taken him? If so, then I needed to react fast, didn't I? Was it already too late?

Oh, my God. I'll have to tell Sophia if he's missing. It'll crush her. I need to find him.

"Now, let's just take it easy," my dad continued.

"Yes, let's' wait and see," my mom continued.

I stared at them. "Wait and see? Wait for what? For his picture to be shoved under the door?"

"Now, Emma," my dad said. "We don't know that this killer-person has taken him. I mean, the door was locked. Can't he have wandered off on his own? Maybe he went on an adventure on the ship."

"That's not very like Christoffer," I said. "He's very responsible." I could hear my voice was shaking. I couldn't just stand here while Sophia's son might be in danger. I had to do something. I was responsible for him.

"I'll go look for him," I said.

"I'll go with you," my dad said. "Four eyes are better than two."

"Someone has to stay here with Victor and in case he comes back on his own," my mom said. "I'll do that."

I stormed out the door with my dad following me. "So where do we start?" my dad asked.

"I have an idea," I said. I ran towards the stairs and took them two steps at a time until I reached the deck below ours. My dad followed me closely.

"Where are we going?" my dad asked, panting.

"I don't know just yet. But I have an idea where his kidnapper might be. Follow me. My guess is, he's on the pool deck."

I found the entrance to the pool deck and ran through the glass doors. I scanned the area quickly and spotted the photographer on the other side. He was talking to a family of four, then he took a picture of them.

"I always thought there was something odd about this guy," I said and walked quickly towards him. "I mean, look at how he dresses. Who wears a black coat outside when it's eighty degrees?"

I ran up to the man and threw myself at him. "Where is he?" I yelled, while grabbing his coat. "I want him back. Now!"

The man in the black coat held onto his camera like it was his only life-line while I shook him. People surrounding us started to look.

"You took him, didn't you?" I continued. "You killed Alberto Colombo, Francesca Alessandrino, and the guy she was with; I know you did. And you placed those photos underneath their doors, you bastard. Why did you even do that? To make them suffer, huh? To let them know how powerful you are? That you decide who will live and who will die? Is that it? Is it a power trip?"

The photographer tried to fight me off and break loose. I held on to him, then tackled his legs so he fell onto the deck. I placed my foot on his neck and held him down. People had started gathering around us.

"Where is he? Where is Christoffer?" I yelled. "Tell me where he is!"

"I don't know where he is," the photographer moaned. "I have no idea what you're talking about."

I sat on his back and held his head into the pavement of the pool deck. "I don't believe you. You took him. Where is he?"

The photographer was about to answer me, when the sound of something approaching in the air drowned out every word. I looked up and saw a huge helicopter floating over our heads. It had the word Polizia written on its side.

46

APRIL 2014

"Right on time," I muttered, as the Italian police came onboard the ship. They sprang out of the helicopter when it landed on the helipad on the tip of the ship.

An officer with very blue eyes came towards me, flanked by four other officers. Between them walked a guy I thought I had seen before and, as they came closer, I realized where.

The surveillance camera! He's the guy that was with Francesca!

I couldn't believe he was alive. But what did it mean?

"What is going on here?" the officer with the very blue eyes asked as he approached me.

I looked down at the photographer beneath me. I was still sitting on his back. "This man has kidnapped a boy. I believe he killed three...uh, two passengers onboard and that he is planning on killing this boy too. I'm responsible for the boy."

"Let us take care of this," the officer said and signaled for me to get up. He grabbed the photographer by the neck and pulled him up. The guy from the surveillance camera stepped forward.

"Is this him?" The blue-eyed officer asked.

The guy shook his head. He was wearing a patch to cover his right eye.

The officer turned to look at me. Then he stepped up on a table and looked at the entire crowd.

"My name is Officer Del Rossi. This man, Mr. Ferdinando Cirillo has told us he was pushed in the water from this ship by another man. The coast guard found Mr. Cirillo when they were looking for Francesca Alessandrino, who was believed to have fallen in also, but now we have reason to believe she has probably been killed aboard this ship."

The crowd gasped. People looked at each other then at Officer Del Rossi for explanation.

"Now, now," he said. "We don't know exactly what has been going on. That is why we are here. Mr. Cirillo believes he can identify the man who pushed him and we believe he is the same man that has abducted Francesca Alessandrino. We ask of all of you to remain calm and cooperative when we start to search the ship. We will be asking a lot of questions and no one will be spared until we have our man. As you may or may not have noticed, this ship stopped sailing on our orders and will now stay here until we have found our man. No one enters this ship and, most importantly, no one leaves. Thank you for your cooperation."

The officer looked at me, then at the photographer next to me. "Now you two. Explain what is going on, please."

"I don't know," the photographer said. "She suddenly attacked me, claiming I had her son."

"He's not my son. He's a friend of my son's. But I'm responsible for him," I said.

"Do you have her son?" Officer Del Rossi asked.

"He is not my...," I gave up. What did it matter if they thought he was my son? As long as we found him. Hopefully alive.

The photographer shook his head.

"He uses Polaroid," I said. "Just like the ones that were pushed under the door of Mr. and Mrs. Alessandrino and the Colombo's door."

Officer Del Rossi looked at me. He squinted his eyes. "You know about the photos? And you say the Colombos also received a photograph?"

"Yes. I found it in their room. Mrs. Colombo had left it in the safe before she took the gun out."

"In the safe you say? What were you doing in their safe, might I ask?" Officer Del Rossi asked suspiciously.

I exhaled. "I was looking for the photo...I really don't have the time for this. I need to find the boy before he is killed...it might even already be too late. I need you to search this man's quarters for me." I pointed at the photographer.

"I don't have him. I told you," he argued.

"We'll see," Officer Del Rossi said. He signaled his colleagues, "We'll start in his cabin. You, the one with the camera. You show us the way."

47

APRIL 1984

The twins didn't sleep much that night after the visit from the men in white coats. They had no idea what to do. It was frustrating.

Their arms and legs were still strapped down. There was no way they'd be able to escape. There wasn't even a window in the room and the door was locked. In the darkness of the cruel night, they wondered what to do. They both knew they would fight this separation with all they had in them. They were joined together for a reason. They were born this way and didn't know anything else.

"I can't live without you, Deedee."

"And I can't imagine a life without you, Dumdum."

"God wanted us to be this way. He created us like this. No one has the right to separate us," Deedee said.

"Or to question our right to live like this," Dumdum said. "We are two separate beings. Though living in the same body, we have two minds."

"It's unfair to lump us together as one," Dumdum said.

"But yet, we belong together," Deedee said. "Why can't they see that? Why don't they understand we need to be joined together, that neither of us can live without the other?"

"They're afraid of us, Deedee," Dumdum said. "We make them uncomfortable. They don't like to look at us. They want to make us be and look like them. Like normal people."

Deedee started sobbing. "I can't believe they'll do this to us. Don't we have anything to say about it? Can't we stop them Dumdum? Can't we?"

"We have to. We have to, somehow," Dumdum answered. "There must be a way. But we must promise each other one thing. If we're ever separated. We must always find each other."

"I promise to find you," Deedee said, with tears in his voice. "I will not leave your side. Not ever. Life is not worth living without you."

The twins went quiet. They wanted to wrap their arms around each other like they used to do as children, but couldn't. Instead, they put their faces really close so their noses touched and fell asleep.

Two hours later, the door to their small room was opened and an army of men and women in white coats entered. They walked to the bed and started unstrapping their arms and legs. As soon as they were loose, the twins started fighting. They kicked and screamed, slamming their fists in the people's faces while growling and snarling. But the men were strong. They held onto them and put them onto a stretcher, where they were strapped down again. Tweedledee and Tweedledum screamed at the top of their lungs while they were being transported down a narrow hallway with bright lights shining in their eyes. They were scared, terrified. Their stretcher was rolled into another room with more bright lights and many instruments. A woman had a syringe in her hand.

"Hurry up," one of the men who had held them down said. "They're like wild beasts."

The woman smiled and lifted the syringe. "This will put an end to all of that," she said. She walked closer to the boys. The men held them down. The boys screamed and growled. Deedee managed to kick one of the men in the head. He fell backwards. Another man tried to hold their arms down, but Dumdum managed to knock him out. Yet another received a punch to his jaw. The twins were growling and fighting. The woman with the syringe fought to get room to put the needle in their skin. But the twins writhed and tossed so much, it was impossible.

"Hold it down!" she hissed.

The twins kicked and hit someone again. With their almost supernatural strength, they managed to pull themselves up and, by some miracle, the straps on their arms were loosened. Maybe from the tossing and writhing, maybe from their strength, or maybe because the straps weren't very strong, but they burst and suddenly the twins were free. They jumped to their arms and hissed at the woman, who backed up with a loud whimper. Then they jumped out of the room and ran on their hands towards the front door of the hospital...Seeing nothing but the ray of sunlight coming through the glass doors. Behind them, people were yelling and screaming for someone to stop them. But the twins didn't care. Beyond that door was freedom. Behind that glass they could run into the world again and be left alone.

"We're free! No one will stop us again," Deedee whined in joy. "No one will ever hurt us again."

At first, they thought something had bitten them, but they both knew the truth. They had experienced this pain before and recognized it...The pain from the arrow of the tranquilizer-gun. They both screamed and looked at each other as their limbs slowly refused to cooperate and they tumbled to the ground, flat on their faces.

Deedee smiled at Dumdum. "I'll find you," he whispered.

"I love you," Dumdum whispered back.

"I love you more."

48

APRIL 2014

The photographer was told to open the door to his cabin. He fumbled with the card in the reader. I noticed he was shaking heavily.

I wasn't doing too well myself. I kept wondering if Christoffer was still alive, or if we were too late. Did he kill his victims right away, then take the picture and get rid of them? He would have to act fast, wouldn't he? In order to for no one to find out.

My heart was thudding in my chest and I had to take deep breaths to calm myself down while we waited for the photographer to get his act together and open the door. The card wouldn't work. Of course, at an important moment like this, the card refused to cooperate. The light above the reader kept flashing red.

"Try again," Officer Del Rossi said.

The photographer tried again and, finally, he succeeded. The lamp flashed green and was accompanied by the well-known click. I closed my eyes for just a second, trying hard to erase the pictures in my mind of what might have happened to Christoffer. What was I going to find on the other side of this door? Did I want to see it? Was it best if I didn't? I swallowed hard and opened my eyes. No. I wanted to know.

Officer Del Rossi grabbed the door handle and walked inside, flanked by two of his men. He ordered them to start the search. I walked inside behind them.

"Christoffer?" I called, my voice trembling with fear. "Are you in here, buddy?"

There was no answer and hope left my body. The officers examined the room, turned over pillows and looked under the bed. I stared at the photographer. He was standing with his head bowed, staring at the floor. On his wall hung hundreds of pictures. I took a closer look at them.

"Why do you have all these pictures of people on the ship?" Officer Del Rossi asked, pointing at them.

"Those are all the ones that no one wanted to buy," he said. "People often say they want me to take a picture, but then, when I show it to them, they don't want it after all. Then I don't get paid."

"But, why keep the pictures? Why hang them on your wall? They're of no value to you. You don't know these people," I said.

"I don't have a family. These are my family."

I bit my lip. The photographer lifted his eyes and looked into mine. I saw something in them. Something I didn't want to see.

"Hm," I said, looking over the pictures. Some of them were quite good, I had to admit.

One of the police officers yelled in Italian from the bathroom. Officer Del Rossi looked at me.

"Has he found something?" I asked.

"Yes, come with me," Officer Del Rossi said.

I stormed into the bathroom, then stopped. Inside, stood the officer who had yelled. He was still speaking in agitated Italian and pointing to the floor. I looked down and saw something that made my heart stop.

It was a huge lock of Christoffer's hair. I recognized the color and the curls. Christoffer liked to keep his hair fairly long. The hair was spread over the floor. I gasped for air.

"It's...It's...it's his," I stuttered.

Tears were welling up in my eyes. A lump in my throat threatened to burst. I kept thinking about Sophia. Could it be? Was he really...? Had this man really done this?

I kneeled next to the hair, while tears rolled down my cheeks. Then I rose to my feet and jumped the photographer.

"You bastard! What did you do to Christoffer?"

49

APRIL 2014

The man was breathing heavily while cleaning his hands. Blood was running of his skin into the white sink. He rubbed some off and put on more soap to get the rest off. He was panting with exhaustion and because of the excruciating pain in his shoulder. He turned the water off, then looked in the mirror.

"I told you, Deedee. It was all worth it."

"I'm so happy you did it, but you're in pain. You're sweating," Deedee answered.

"It doesn't matter. Having you close is all that matters. Feeling you up there, seeing you looking back at me in the mirror is all worth it."

"It feels good," Deedee said. "I like it up here."

The man forced a smile. Looking at Deedee's head that he had sewn back onto his shoulder made him happy. Even if the infection had gotten worse, even if the pain was increasing. The area around the head was swollen and red. It was throbbing.

The man took a deep breath, then turned to look at the boy who was still sleeping on his bed.

"Now, let's get you a new face."

He knew he had to hurry and started to pull out instruments from his bag. He placed them neatly in a row on the white paper towel.

"They're on to us, Deedee," he said. "They will soon be looking for us."

The man had seen the helicopter arrive and knew he was running out of time. But he had bought himself a little more time. He had seen the woman, the boy's mother fight the photographer on the pool deck. He knew he could use that for something. So he had gone back and cut a lock of hair from the boy, then run to the photographer's cabin and hidden his little surprise for them. He had placed it strategically where he knew they wouldn't miss it.

Actually, it was all Deedee's idea. He was the clever one of the two. He could come up with things like that.

"That should keep them busy for a couple of hours," he said, when he told the man about his plan.

The man had thought it was brilliant.

The boy on the bed was still sleeping heavily. The man suddenly wondered if he had used too high of a dose. After all, he had no idea what the boy weighed. He appeared heavier than he was, he now realized. He was tall, but very scrawny. It would take longer than anticipated for him to wake up.

"Should we just do it while he's asleep?" Deedee asked.

"No! I want to look into his eyes before I kill him. You know I want to. That's what I have to do; I need that and you know it," the man hissed. Then he regretted his outburst. "I'm sorry Deedee. I'm a little tense, that's all. I didn't mean to be angry with you."

The man heard loud voices and footsteps in the hallway outside his door. He used the peephole to look out. The hallway was crowded. People were talking loudly. He spotted the woman. She seemed agitated. She was being held back by two police officers, while that photographer-fool was being held by two others. He was wearing handcuffs. And—*oh the joy*—he was bleeding. The uniformed men walked with strong forceful and serious steps towards his door. Then he gasped. Someone was with them.

Oh no. This isn't good.

Could it be? Was it really? It was. It was him! It was the guy the man had thrown over the railing the other night. He was wearing a patch over his eye where the man had burned him with his cigarette. The man started sweating again. How was this possible? How had he survived? The man drew in a couple of deep breaths to calm himself.

"He saw my face. He knows who I am," he mumbled.

This is not the time to panic. You have to stay focused.

The man held his breath and listened to their words. It was the woman who did most of the talking. She was telling them about the photographs and how she had a hunch that Mrs. Colombo had killed herself and that was why she went to examine her suite on her own and found the picture in the safe. Then she yelled at the photographer.

"Tell me what you did to him, you bastard!"

They were passing his door. The man was watching them closely.

"They're doing just as I expected," he mumbled. "You can't see it Deedee, but I'm telling you. They took the bait."

"I knew they would," Deedee said. "I knew they'd find your present."

"I placed it in his bathroom...On the floor, next to the shower. Of course they'd find it. I wasn't worried at all."

The man left the peephole as the last of the crowd passed his door. With a deep sigh of relief, he returned to face the boy, just as he started squinting his eyes.

"He's waking up," Deedee said.

The man grabbed his coat and put it on. He sat on the edge of the bed while smiling. "I know Deedee. I know. It's time."

50

APRIL 2014

My dad had gone back to my suite when the police told him he wasn't allowed to walk with us down to the photographer's cabin. He was the first person I saw when I opened the door after being escorted back by the officers. He could tell by the look in my eyes that something was wrong. I threw myself in his arms.

"What happened, sweetie?"

My mother was standing behind him, biting her nails.

Finally, I let it all out. I sobbed, I cried. "Oh Dad. You won't believe it. It's horrible."

"What happened? Did they find him?" my dad asked. "Was Christoffer down there?"

My entire body was shaking and my knees collapsed beneath me. My dad grabbed me and held me in his arms. He carried me to the couch.

"Where is Christoffer?" he asked.

"We don't know. But he had him. He has him somewhere. We just don't know where," I said, crying loudly. I looked into my dad's eyes, then burst into tears again.

"How do you know he has him?" my mother asked.

"Because...because we found a lock of his hair. It was in the bathroom."

My mother covered her mouth. "Oh, my God."

My dad slammed his fist into the couch. "The bastard!" He looked at me again. "But that doesn't mean he's dead, does it? I mean you didn't find...you didn't find Christoffer, did you?"

"No. We still don't know what he's done to him. They took him away for interrogation. Hopefully, they'll find out soon, they said. They escorted me back here and told me I had to wait. I think I hurt the guy when I attacked him down there. I bit his nose. He was bleeding heavily afterwards. I just got so angry. You wouldn't believe it, Dad. I was so angry."

"Oh, I believe it," he said. "I'd do something similar if I could get my hands on the bastard. No doubt about it. If he's hurt the boy in any way, I'll...I'll..."

"I know, Dad."

"Was there any blood?" my mother asked.

"What?" I looked at Victor who, once again, had his nose buried in Christoffer's book. He didn't seem to notice any of the turmoil going on around him.

My mother cleared her throat. "Was there any blood in the cabin? Anything in the bathroom?" she asked.

I shook my head. "No. Only the hair."

"Isn't that a little odd?" she asked.

I frowned. "No. He must have washed everything down or something."

"And left a big lock of hair on the floor?" my mother continued.

I was getting annoyed with her. Why did she all of a sudden feel like being a detective?

"He did it. I know he took him, Mom," I snapped at her.

"Your mother's right," my dad said. "At least no blood is good news. And if he was careful enough to clean the place for blood, he would have seen the hair. Don't you think?"

I shrugged. "Maybe."

"So maybe there is a small chance that he never hurt Christoffer?" my mother said. "Maybe he is just hiding him somewhere."

"It's small, but it is a hope," my dad said and put his hand in mine.

I bit my lip, wondering if they could be right. Was there a slight hope still? Part of me was afraid to believe it. Part of me was terrified not to.

"They told me they'd let me know as soon as they knew anything," I said, while snorting. "Until then, I'm not allowed to leave my suite. They're afraid I might do something to ruin their investigation, like destroy important evidence. But I hate waiting. I hate not being able to do anything," I said, sobbing. "If Christoffer is still alive somewhere on this ship, I need to find him. He must be terrified. I know I am."

51

APRIL 1984

Tweedledum opened his eyes and looked at the white ceiling. He felt strange. He moved his body a little to the side and looked down. Then he gasped. He turned his head frantically in the direction where Deedee used to be. But the other side of the bed was empty.

Oh, my God. Oh, my God. I'm all alone!

Dumdum started sobbing, while calling for his twin brother. "Deedee, Deedee where are you?"

This feeling of being all alone was painful. It was so wrong. So strange and so inconceivable. Dumdum cried. He couldn't take it. He couldn't bear being left like this...this silence, this solitude...no sound of someone else moving or breathing close to him.

"Deedee," he cried into the empty room. "You promised you'd never leave me. You promised!"

I can't believe he is gone. I can't believe I'm all alone. I don't want to be alone. We've always been together. We've done everything together. Please, don't leave me. Please find me.

Dumdum sobbed when the door suddenly opened and a man entered. Dumdum recognized him by his grey beard. He was smiling.

"You're awake," he said.

Dumdum yelled at him in his and Deedee's secret language.

"Now, now," the man said. "No need to yell. There is no room for your aggressive behavior in this place," he said and wrote on his pad.

"Deedee," Dumdum yelled. "Deedee?"

"Oh your brother? Well...I'm sorry to have to tell you this, but he didn't make it. He was too weak. You were always the strong one. We could only save you. I have to say it hurts me badly. I want you to know we fought for him as long as we could. But there was no chance. I'm sorry for your loss. I can tell you, the doctor who performed the surgery, Dr. Alessandrino, has taken the failure very hard. He has resigned from the hospital."

The man with the beard cleared his throat. Tweedledum was in shock. He stared at the man, while groaning and trying to pull himself loose from his straps.

"Now I want us to start all over," the man said. "My name is Dr. D'Avanzo. I will be your doctor and be the one to help you get back to a normal life. I have high hopes for you and think that you and I can make real progress here."

Tweedledum snarled. Then he barked and snapped his teeth at the doctor.

"Of course, if it turns out you refuse to cooperate, then we will have to utilize other methods," the doctor said.

Tweedledum didn't stop. He kept barking like a dog at the doctor, wanting to hurt him, to kill him for what he had done. The sorrow in Dumdum's heart was so painful.

"Very well," the doctor said and pushed a button on the wall. Soon after, the room was filled with men and women wearing the same white coats.

"This patient suffers from a severe case of schizophrenia after the loss of his brother. He is severely delusional and needs help to provide relief from his psychiatric illnesses. Take him to room nine," the doctor instructed them.

Soon Dumdum was rolled down another hallway, while screaming and yelling his pain and sorrow out.

"This will calm you down," the doctor said, as they placed the electrodes on his forehead. "We're only doing it to help you."

Tweedledum still screamed while they strapped him down and gave him the anesthesia. When he woke up again, he didn't scream anymore. After that, they gave him more electroshock-treatments...three times a week. They gave him medicine to calm him down and soon he remembered his brother no more. In fact, he didn't remember anything.

52

APRIL 2014

I called Morten and told him everything. Crying, sobbing, and talking angrily I told him the whole story. He was in shock.

"Oh my God, Emma. That's terrible. You want me to contact the Italian police down there and get involved? I'll do anything. If they're investigating the disappearance of a Danish boy, they should have backup from us."

"I don't know if it'll help anything, but it probably won't hurt anything either. So that would be nice. Thank you."

"No problem. I'm going to book a plane ticket and come down there. Where are you now?" he asked.

"I have no idea. We left Sorrento and sailed all day yesterday, but today we've been still most of the day. I have no idea how far we've come or where we'll dock next. They're not being very informative. Most people onboard have no clue what's going on. According to the original plan, we were supposed to dock in Sicily tonight, but the police told us the ship will stay put until this thing has been solved. They don't want anyone to be able to leave the ship."

"So, I'll book a flight to Rome, then decide what to do once I'm there. You'll probably know more by then," Morten said.

"It's awfully nice of you. Can you afford it?" I asked sniffling.

"It's police-work. I'll be there in the line of duty; the state has to pay for it. Don't you worry about that."

I heard him tapping on his keyboard. It felt so good to talk to him, even if the circumstances were horrifying.

"Let's just see what I can get tonight...there's a flight out at six. I'll be in Rome at eight thirty. How does that sound? I'll contact the local police and see how I can be helpful."

"That would be really great. I'm not sure I can do this alone. I feel so... I'm just so...oh God, Morten, what if he already killed Christoffer? What if he just dropped the body somewhere? What if he threw it overboard?" I gasped for air. "How am I ever going to tell Sophia? Should I call her now and tell her he's missing? It'll freak her out. I don't know what to do, Morten."

"Emma, you need to calm yourself down. Don't let your mind get carried away. Where are your mom and dad?"

"They left."

"They left? Now? When you need them the most?" Morten asked.

"Well, I told them to. I told them to search the ship and ask everyone they met if they had seen Christoffer. I can't just sit here, Morten. I have to at least do something. The police told me to not leave my suite while they're interrogating the photographer, so I have to stay here with Victor, but come on. I can't just do nothing!"

"Of course you can't. I can't believe he took Christoffer. Why would he take him? What does he want with his victims? You said he killed a teenage boy and a teenage girl? Is it something sexual? Christoffer isn't a teenager. I don't understand it," Morten said.

"I don't either. Maybe he's just irrational. Maybe he just kills randomly for no particular reason," I said with a sigh. I was tired of crying, sick of feeling helpless.

"Now you're sounding like me," Morten said. "It's usually the other way around."

"I know. I think we've been a couple for too long," I said.

"It feels like déjà-vu all over again, huh?"

"I know. I can't believe it. Why does everything keep happening to me? Is it something I do?"

Morten sighed. "At least it doesn't seem like the killer targeted you this time. It doesn't seem planned. There doesn't seem to be an ulterior motive."

"That's true. At least not one I can find. He takes photos of people, then kidnaps their kids. No bodies have been found. One guy was thrown in the ocean."

"Hm," Morten said. "That's odd."

"I know. I think he targets these kids and the guy must have gotten in his way somehow. That's my theory."

"And he sends the parents photos, you say?" Morten asked pensively.

"Yes. Both sets of parents received a photo stuck underneath their door."

"What was in the photos?"

"One showed Alberto Colombo lying on his back with dead empty eyes. His chest and stomach had been flayed."

"Flayed you say? Huh?"

"Yes." The image has stayed with me. I gave it back to the police for the investigation, but it still lingers with me.

"And the other one?"

"A chopped off leg," I said.

"Ouch. That's bad."

"I know." I went quiet, thinking about what the photographer could possibly have to send me. "So, what do you make of it?"

"Well, it's messy. What he does is messy. And you say there was no blood in his bathroom. Just a lock of hair?" Morten asked.

"Yes. Just the hair on the floor. But maybe he washed the place down," I said.

"When? When do you suppose he would have had time to do all that?"

"What do you mean?"

"You said you came into the suite and Christoffer was gone. Immediately, you ran to the pool deck and attacked the guy and then the police came and you all went to his cabin on the lower deck where the personnel live."

"Yes...I see what you're getting at..."

"Flaying a person or sawing off their leg takes a long time. And it is very messy."

"So you're saying he didn't do it? Is that it?" I asked.

"Well, maybe he never got to it, but at least that would mean Christoffer was still alive somewhere. He could also have killed him and then hidden him somewhere with the intent of doing his thing to him later. Or maybe he didn't do any of it. Maybe you have the wrong person."

"What about the hair?" I asked, confused. It was all getting a little too much for me right now. Thinking about poor Christoffer being flayed or not was really hard.

"It seems a little odd that he would cut off some hair when he was this pressed for time. I mean, he had to go to your suite, kidnap Christoffer and somehow drag him all the way down to the lower deck, then cut off some of his hair before he rushed up to the pool deck and you could attack him."

"And hide him somewhere. Don't forget that," I said.

"Exactly. It doesn't seem possible. And people would notice a guy with a boy over his shoulder."

"Yeah, but he works here."

"As a photographer. Photographers don't carry people around."

"That's true. So he could have hidden him here somewhere—on the upper deck or close to the pool area," I said, feeling a slight ray of hope grow in me. Morten was right. There was no way he could have done all those things. Maybe he didn't manage to kill Christoffer. Maybe he just sedated him somehow. Maybe he was unconscious and hidden somewhere nearby?

"That could very well be," Morten said.

"Or...," I stopped and looked out the window at the glittering blue ocean.

"Or what?" Morten asked.

"I think I know exactly what to do."

53

APRIL 2014

C hristoffer opened his eyes. He felt weary and his body was sore. He gasped. A strange face was staring at him.

"Who are you?" asked Christoffer with a shaking voice.

The man didn't seem to understand what he was saying. He spoke to him in Italian. Christoffer didn't understand.

"What is this place? Where am I?" Christoffer asked.

The man didn't understand his Danish either. He looked at Christoffer with a tilted head. His eyes were creepy. Christoffer didn't understand what was going on. Where was Emma Frost? Where was Victor? Who was this man in the long black coat?

Christoffer tried to sit up, but the man pushed him down. He switched to English. Christoffer understood a few words. He had never been good at English in school.

"Now, now, my boy. You're not well. Lay still."

Not well? Am I sick? I don't understand. Mommy what is this?

Christoffer felt tears in his eyes. "I want to call my mom," he said. He tried to sit up again, but the man pushed him back down.

"Stay in bed, please," the man said. "Doctor's orders!"

Then he giggled. Christoffer didn't like the way he laughed or looked at him.

"I have to get back," Christoffer said.

"No, no, no," the doctor said, with his pointer finger in the air and a strange smile on his face. Suddenly, Christoffer remembered where he had seen him before. On the deck on the first day when they waved at the people back at the quay.

Christoffer looked behind the man and suddenly spotted instruments on the table, nicely lined up. They looked like the ones he had seen in Victor's strange books. Knives and scalpels. What was he going to do with them?

Christoffer gasped for air while he spoke. "What...what is that?" he asked. His voice was trembling heavily. "What are you going to do with those?"

Christoffer pointed at the table behind the man. The man turned and looked. Then he giggled. "Ah those," he said. "You're wondering about them. Beautiful aren't they? Don't worry. I cleaned them well."

Christoffer didn't understand much of what he said. He was scared, terrified. He tried, once again, to get up, but the man forced him down again. This time, he slapped him across the face.

"No getting up," he said. "Stay in bed."

Christoffer touched his cheek. It was throbbing. Then he cried. "Please, sir. Please just let me get back to my friends. I miss my mom. Please, let me go."

The man tilted his head again and Christoffer knew he didn't understand his Danish. He was sobbing now. How was he supposed to explain to the man that he wanted to go back? His cheek was hurting badly. The man was giggling and looking at him strangely. He reached down and grabbed his face between his fingers and pulled the skin on his cheeks. Then he laughed and nodded.

"Very nice. Very soft and smooth," the man said.

"Please, sir," Christoffer pleaded. Tears were rolling quickly down his cheeks. The man wiped them off with a napkin. Then he smiled.

"Before we start, there's someone I want you to meet," he said.

Christoffer didn't want to. He wanted to get out of this place. He wanted to go back to the suite where he had fallen asleep. He wanted his mom.

Help me, Mommy. Help me. This is a very bad man. I think he is a very bad man, Mommy.

The man rose and pulled off his black coat with a grin.

"Meet Deedee," he said. "Deedee, meet your new face."

Christoffer looked at the strange thing that seemed to be sewn to the man's shoulder. What was that? Christoffer gasped for air.

Mommy, the bad man has a head on his shoulder. It's creepy.

The man took one of the knives from the table. He leaned in over Christoffer, who was sweating and shaking.

"I'm sorry. This will hurt a lot," he said. He lifted Christoffer's chin so he looked into the man's eyes.

Just as he placed the knife on Christoffer's throat, there was a loud knock on the door.

54

FEBRUARY 1980

Salvatore Rosetti had thought about his babies every day, every hour of his life since he left them in the dumpster. For many years, he drank the pain away, traveling the seas working as a sailor doing any kind of job they would let him. The harder, the better, since it seemed to make him forget the pain slightly, at least for a short while, the harder he worked.

But it never lasted long before it was back to torture him.

Once land-bound again, ten years later, he tried another approach. He visited his childhood church outside of Rome and asked father Adorno for forgiveness. He told him everything about the babies that he hadn't wanted and that he had regretted abandoning for every minute since.

"I even went back there, Father," he said, sitting in the confession chair. "Later that same night, I returned. But the dumpster was empty. They were gone. I keep picturing what might have happened to them. I keep wondering if an animal, a fox or maybe something bigger might have taken them."

Father Adorno thought it over for a little while. "Or maybe a kind and merciful human took them in. Did you ever think about that?"

"You mean to say, they might still be alive?" Salvatore had never dared to think the thought, but now it sparkled inside of him, this newfound hope that maybe, just maybe, they were out there somewhere.

"They might be," the father said.

"I need to find them," he said.

"First, you must repent, my son."

"Do you think God will ever forgive me?"

"I believe he will. But you must ask him to. And you must repent your sins first."

"I repent. I repent," Salvatore said.

After leaving the church, Salvatore realized he had no way of knowing where to start looking. He decided to start where it had all begun. At the dumpster in the alley. Salvatore made posters and placed them all over the area and, every day, he waited by the dumpster like he had said on the poster that he would, hoping someone would show up.

After three days, someone did. An old woman who told him she lived in the building next to the alley.

"I saw your boys," she said. "I found them when I was throwing out my trash one night. I gave them to the orphanage. If you're lucky, they still have them there."

Tears rolled quickly down Salvatore's face. He looked at the woman with compassion. He grabbed her hand and shook it eagerly. "Thank you, thank you so much. Thank you for taking them."

Then he ran off to the orphanage. He asked about the boys, but the manager told him they had run off many years ago.

"Four years, I believe it is," she said. "They stole money from me and we haven't seen them since. My guess is, they were killed in the streets. Freaks like them won't last long out there. My advice to you Mr. Rosetti, is to simply let it go. Forget about them. Find a nice wife and have some other children. It's not too late for a man like you."

Salvatore felt sick to his stomach. They weren't there anymore? They had run away? Did that mean he had lost their trail? Did he have to give up already? Salvatore decided he wasn't going to.

My boys are out there and they need me. I know I have done them wrong, but it is never too late to repent. I can correct what has been done wrong. I can make it up to them. There is nothing time cannot erase. God will help me find them. No matter the cost.

But Salvatore had no money and, soon, the search for the children became too expensive for him. He had to find a place to live and a job. One day, Salvatore was walking the streets, looking for his twins, when he spotted a man lying in the street holding a hand to his chest.

"What happened?" he said and ran to him.

The man fainted just as Salvatore got there. Salvatore had learned CPR onboard one of the ships, from the chef. It was important that they knew how to help each other in case of an emergency. On the tankers, they could often travel for weeks without seeing land and they were always far from a doctor.

So with this knowledge, Salvatore performed CPR on the man and, soon, he came back to life. He sat up and coughed. Then he turned to look at Salvatore.

"You saved my life," he said. "Not many people would help a man in need in the streets. I have a heart condition. Could you help me get home to my medicine?"

Salvatore helped the elderly man get back. He helped him find his pills and found water for him to drink. Afterwards, the man looked at him and said:

"I can tell you enjoy taking care of others. I believe you would make an excellent doctor. If you'd like to become one, I would love to train you in the medical field. I'll pay for your schooling. What do you say?"

55

APRIL 2014

The man groaned, annoyed, as he ran up the stairs, not bothering to wait for the elevator. He had to put on his black coat to hide Deedee and he had no time to remove the stitches and take him off. Plus, he needed him to be on his shoulder when he flayed the boy.

The boy, oh yes, how he looked forward to cutting off his scalp.

"Such a pretty face, Deedee. So perfect. Such a beautiful skin. You're going to be so beautiful," he mumbled, as he ran across the hall with his brown bag in his hand. The wound on his shoulder was hurting, and he had to take a couple of pills to help with the pain.

"So pretty, Deedee. You'll be perfect. Just you wait and see."

The man had sedated the boy again to make sure he didn't run anywhere while he did what he had to.

"Of all times, why did they need me now?" he mumbled. "I was in the middle of something. Why did they come knocking on my door just now?"

He stopped in front of a door, then took in a deep breath to calm himself. Then he knocked. The woman opened the door.

The man smiled. "Someone called for a doctor?"

"Yes," the woman said and stepped aside to let the man inside. "I did. I'm Emma Frost. Come on in."

The man walked inside. He was getting tired of this woman.

Maybe you should kill her while you're here. Get rid of her. She's annoying.

You're right, Deedee. You're right. She's in my way.

"So, what is the emergency?" he asked and looked to see if there was anyone else in the room. He spotted the other boy in the living room with his nose stuck in a book.

The woman closed the door. "The emergency you say? Well. Let's see. Maybe the emergency is my son not feeling well, or maybe I'm not feeling well. Oh no, the emergency is, of course, that my friend's son, the boy I'm responsible for is MISSING," Emma Frost yelled.

"Yes, yes. I heard about that," the man said. "Awful. But they caught the guy, didn't they? If you're feeling upset, I can get you something to relax you." The man put the brown bag on the dresser. He bent over it and opened it.

"Oh, I don't think I need to relax," she said. "But I do think you have him."

The man didn't look up. "What was that? I'm not sure I understood that last part," he lied.

"It was something my friend said when I was on the phone with him just now," she continued. "He said that a photographer couldn't get away with carrying a young boy around on the ship. But then I realized that someone else could get away with that without anyone raising an eyebrow. A doctor could. What did you use? A stretcher, right? You sedated your victims and took them to your cabin on a stretcher, right?"

The man laughed and shook his head. He grabbed the scalpel from his bag. "Now...I really have to say...," he turned his head and looked at her. He could smell her fear from across the room. Maybe this could be fun after all. It was always more fun to kill someone who was afraid.

"It's true, right? You did it...Oh, my God. Now I know where I've seen you before," Emma Frost said. "The black coat, the hat. You were on the deck on the first day we were here. You asked me about the boys. Did you... were you checking them out? Was that when you decided to take Christoffer? Was it, huh? Where is he? What have you done with him?"

"Now, let's not argue," the man said.

"What was your name again?" she asked.

The man hid the scalpel in his hand and moved it to the pocket of his coat. He took a step towards the woman.

"Salvatore, signora. Salvatore Rosetti."

"Well, Salvatore," she said, with the phone in her hand. Salvatore could tell her hand was shaking. It was almost hilarious. Pathetic was maybe a better word.

"I'm calling the police now and will have them come up here. Then you'll show me to Christoffer, do you hear me?" she asked.

Salvatore shook his head. "No, you won't."

56

FEBRUARY 2014

Salvatore Rosetti moved slowly across the graveyard. The gravedigger walking in front of him showed him the way.

"It's right over here in the back," he said. "We don't get many visitors all the way back here."

The man stopped in front of a small stone. He sniffled and wiped his nose on his sleeve. It was a cold winter day and a thick fog had refused to leave the town all morning. Salvatore shuddered in his black coat.

"Here it is," the man said. "All they told us was to write Tweedledee on the stone. The hospital told us that was his name. They never knew his last name." He patted Salvatore on the shoulder. "Well, I'll leave you two alone."

He sniffled again, then walked away. Salvatore didn't even look after him. To him, he was unimportant. Salvatore kneeled in front of the grave, then burst into tears. He placed his hand on the stone and read the one single word.

"Tweedledee."

He wept loudly. Twenty-four years of searching for the twins had led him to this place. It was almost unbearable. For years, he had traced the twins' whereabouts across town. He had learned about the policeman who had forced them to do dogfights, he learned about the gypsies who beat them and displayed them publically all over the country, only to end up being killed where it all began by the ones they had tortured. He had been thrilled to know that the boys had been able to stand up for themselves, that they had killed the gypsies. But after that, he had lost their trail. For many years, there were no results to his search. All he knew was that they had lived in the streets for years, but suddenly, one day, they were gone. Probably been killed, most people said. But Salvatore hadn't believed them. He refused to. They had killed the gypsies. Massacred them, one after another. They could defend themselves.

While searching for their whereabouts, Salvatore had gone through med-school and ended up working for the old man whose life he saved, working in his private clinic. On the day the old man died and left his clinic to Salvatore, the closest he ever came to having a son; Salvatore sold the clinic and spent most of the money on his endless search. Finally, when he needed to get a new job, he read in the paper that one of the cruise ships had a position open for a doctor. Missing the great ocean and the solitude of being on the sea, Salvatore decided to take it. He would look for the boys on his weeks off. It was perfect.

But the search yielded nothing for years. Not until December 2013, when Salvatore finally had a breakthrough. A former nurse responded to his ad in the newspaper and told him she had seen his boys, that they had been in the hospital where she worked. Salvatore visited the hospital and found the old files.

"They were separated?" he asked the doctor in charge, who gave him the files.

"I'm afraid so," she said.

"How? Who authorized it?"

"Doctor Alessandrino," she said. "He was in charge of the hospital in the eighties. He resigned after the operation went wrong."

"Went wrong?" Salvatore asked.

"He lost one of the twins. The other went mad from the loss, unfortunately."

Salvatore bent forward like he was in serious pain. "He lost him?"

"Yes. I'm afraid Tweedledee died in 1984. Tweedledum is still in a home outside of town. But, I have to warn you. They performed a lobotomy on him in 1986 and he is not aware of his surroundings. He will not know who you are."

Salvatore had visited Tweedledum in the home and cried while holding his hand. But it was like he was already dead. He didn't even look at him. Now, Salvatore had finally found Tweedledee's grave and, finally, he could cry out his sorrow and pain.

"I'm so sorry," he wept. "It's all my fault. The way it ended it was all my fault. If only I hadn't left you that day. If only I had..."

Salvatore wept and sobbed. His salty tears hit the dirt beneath him and, as he watched them wet the ground, he was certain he heard a voice call for him.

"Papà is that you? Is that you Papà?"

"Deedee? Is that you?"

"Yes, Papà. I'm down here, but it's so dark. I can't see anything. I can't see you."

Salvatore spotted a shovel by the wall and grabbed it. He started digging in the grave until the case appeared. He threw himself at it and wiped it clean. Then he opened it. The stench was appalling, but the sight was all he had been looking for.

In there, was his son. The skin had rotted away and he was nothing but bones.

"I'm sorry, Deedee. I'm so sorry. I'll make it up to you," Salvatore sobbed. "I'll give you anything you need."

"I'm glad you came, Papà. I'm so glad you're finally here."

"So am I, son. So am I. From now on, everything will be fine. I promise you."

57

APRIL 2014

"**Y**ES, **I** WILL."

I looked at the doctor in front of me. He was walking slowly towards me with a weird and creepy smile on his face.

"I'll call the police right now," I said. I hoped he wouldn't see it on my face, but I had already called Officer Del Rossi earlier and told him I believed the doctor had Christoffer.

"The doctor, aha," Del Rossi had replied. "We'll take a look at him as soon as we're done with the first man you claimed had him."

I had hung up, thinking it would be too late and that I had to do something on my own. I wasn't allowed to leave my suite, so I thought I'd bring the doctor here instead.

Dr. Rosetti was shivering as he walked. He was sweating, but looked like he was cold. Why was he wearing that big coat anyway? Come to think of it, he didn't look very well. He looked like he was sick or something.

"Before you do anything. There is someone you simply have to meet," he said with a grin.

While I dialed the number to the ship's operator, he grabbed the edge of his coat and pulled it off.

I gasped and immediately dropped the phone, as I clapped both my hands to my mouth. The doctor picked it up.

"What the hell is that?" I screamed.

"Emma Frost, meet Deedee. Deedee, meet Emma Frost."

I stared at the head sewn onto Dr. Rosetti's shoulder. It was so repulsive. A skull that had been patched up with pieces of skin and attempted to be sewn together. It was sewn onto Dr. Rosetti's shoulder. The wound surrounding where it had been sewn on was bleeding and looked swollen. The skin around it was bloody and a yellow infection ran out from it. It was nauseating to look at and the smell was even worse.

"That is sickening."

"Well, I admit he needs a little work and that is where your boy comes in. I need his face for my Deedee. Deedee needs a new face, right Deedee?"

He's even talking to it?

"Yes, Papà, I need a new face."

He is answering too. Of course he is.

I started backing up slowly, realizing how sick this person in front of me really was. "So you've been patching up...uh...Deedee with the skin from others?" I asked, while looking for some kind of weapon to defend myself with.

"Yes, yes. That's correct!" he said chirping happily. "Emma Frost understands. She gets us, Deedee. She understands."

"She is so smart, Papà."

"That she is."

I stared at the guy having a conversation with the skull on his shoulder. It had to be the strangest thing I had ever seen. And I had seen a lot.

I fumbled backwards and touched the wall, then slid slowly to the side to see if I could get to the door to the bedroom and maybe hide in there. Maybe find something to hurt him with, or maybe just find my cellphone. It was in there on the nightstand.

"Too bad she has to die, Deedee. Too bad."

"Just don't hurt her pretty face, Papà."

"I won't," he said and pulled out the scalpel from his pocket. He stormed towards me and I shrieked in fear. I managed to duck down just in time and the scalpel landed in the wall, cutting up the nice, and probably expensive, painting of a beach chair and hat.

Dr. Rosetti grunted, then reached down and grabbed me by the throat. He was panting and growling as he pulled me up and held me against the wall.

"She's fast, Deedee. But not fast enough."

"Not fast enough, Papà."

Dr. Rossetti stared into my eyes with such strong anger and hatred, it scared me senseless. "Please," I said.

His grip tightened around my neck. I could hardly breathe. I gasped and sputtered. "Pleeas..."

There was a strange sound...Like the cracking of a melon. Suddenly, the doctor's eyes changed drastically. His facial expression froze. Blood sputtered out of his mouth and onto my face. Then the grip on my neck loosened and I fell to the ground with him on top of me and the patched-up skull fell onto my face. I screamed and pushed it away.

Then I saw him.

"Victor!"

He was standing behind the doctor. His hand was still holding onto the shaft of the axe that was now in the doctor's back. Blood had spurted onto his face. Behind Victor, glass was shattered all over the floor.

"The fire axe," I stuttered and got up.

Victor was staring at the dead doctor and paid no attention to me. I grabbed the phone from the floor and dialed the operator.

58

APRIL 2014

"**WHAT A MESS.**"

Officer Del Rossi scratched his hair underneath his hat. He looked baffled. The doctor was still on the floor of my suite, in a pool of his own blood. Del Rossi had sent his officers downstairs to search the doctor's cabin to find Christoffer. I was still shaking from the attack and fear that something had happened to Christoffer.

Please, let him be alright. Poor boy. Please, tell me he is okay.

"What is that on his shoulder?" he asked.

"I haven't the faintest idea. But he called it Deedee."

"Very well then. We'll have to secure the entire suite and search for evidence."

"What about the boy?" I asked. "What about Christoffer?"

I had barely finished the sentence before Officer Del Rossi's phone rang. He picked it up. "Yes, yes. Oh, you did? Well, excellent."

He put the phone back in his pocket and smiled.

"They found your boy," he said.

I breathed a sigh of great relief. "They found Christoffer? Is he alive?" I asked with my heart in my throat.

"Yes. He was asleep when they got there. They're bringing him back here."

I breathed in relief. I looked at Victor. He was sitting on the couch in the living room, looking at his shoes. I had tried to wash off the blood from his face, but he desperately needed a bath. And I was going to throw away his clothes after this. I had no idea how he was going to react to this. Having killed someone isn't something you just do, then move on as usual afterwards. Even if it was to save the life of your own mother. I was going to have a long talk with him later.

"That is really good news. The doctor didn't hurt him?"

"Not a scratch," was what my men said.

"Good. What a relief."

"Like I said, we'll need to seal off the suite to secure evidence. You'll have to stay somewhere else tonight."

"Well, I hardly think we'll be sleeping in here, even if they clean it up. It just doesn't feel right, if you know what I mean."

"You can sleep in our suite, all three of you."

I turned my head with a smile. "Dad!" I threw myself into his arms.

"Oh, baby. What happened here? What is that on the floor?" My dad turned his head to face my mother, who was standing in the doorway. "Ulla, don't come in here. It's awful. You shouldn't see this." My dad looked down at me. "Are you alright? Is Victor alright?"

"I think we are. Victor did this, Dad. Victor saved me. He took the fire-axe and planted it in the back of the guy."

"Victor did that?" my mother asked. She had stepped inside anyway, curious as she was. She covered her eyes. "That is really nasty."

"Well, I told you," my dad said. "How is Victor?"

"I don't know. He's sitting in there saying nothing. The policeman needs to take his statement, but he refuses to speak. I think I need to get him away from here. But the police need me here. I have to give my statement too."

"Let me take him," my mother said. Without waiting for my reply, she stormed into the living room and sat next to him. She spoke with him for a little while, then took his Pompeii-book in her hand. To my surprise, Victor seemed to listen to her. He got up and walked with her.

"We'll just be in our suite," my mom whispered as she walked past us. "I'll make sure he gets a bath too. Don't worry. You could use one as well, Emma. And a clean shirt. Yours is smeared with blood."

Then she left, with Victor walking right behind her. I was speechless. But also relieved.

"Emma?" a weak voice said behind me.

I turned and looked into Christoffer's gorgeous eyes. He was walking in, flanked by two officers.

"Christoffer!" I grabbed him in my arms the way I always dreamed of grabbing Victor.

"Easy, you're crushing me," he laughed.

I loosened my grip, but didn't let go of him. "I'm so sorry. I'm just so happy to see you again. Don't think I'm ever letting go of you again."

EPILOGUE

The trip ended in Sicily. Once the police were done interviewing everyone and examining everything, they allowed the ship to dock in the port of Palermo. Everyone was told to get their things and leave the ship. The cruise line told people to get on a bus and be transported to another ship they had docked close-by. But for me and my family, the trip was over. I was done with sailing and all any of us wanted to do was to go home.

Morten met us in Palermo and we stayed there for four more nights, waiting to get on a flight home. We stayed in a nice small local hotel where the food was great and there was solid ground under our feet. Christoffer was very upset and cried a lot the first day or two. I let him use my phone to talk to his mother as much as he needed to. On the third day, he seemed better and we went to the beach for a couple of hours.

In the afternoon, Officer Del Rossi called me. I was still at the beach and sat under a palm tree while talking to him.

"We know who he was," he said. "Apparently he was the father of a couple of conjoined children from Rome. The one was killed during the attempt to separate them and the other is still in a mental hospital...basically a vegetable. Apparently, Salvatore somehow, we still don't know how, lost them as children and didn't find them again until it was too late. He must have lost it by then and dug up the remains of his son Deedee. Apparently, he sewed the head onto his shoulder, pretending they were conjoined and took it on and off when he needed to. The wound was very infected. The twins were called Tweedledum and Tweedledee, after the nursery rhyme. Just Dumdum and Deedee as nicknames."

"Okay, that makes sense, I guess. And the victims had no connection to the twins after all? They were just random then? Because he wanted their skin?"

"Apparently, he was building a new body for his son. We found remains of what looked like the attempt to make a body or a suit or something made from the skin of his victims. But, not all of the victims were random, we think. Apparently, the Alessandrino's had a connection to the twins. Dr. Alessandrino was the one who separated the twins when one died during the surgery. It harmed his career badly. But, while Francesca Alessandrino was, indeed, planned, the rest seem to be random victims."

"He wanted the doctor to suffer for what he had done to his boys. He wanted them to feel the same pain he had felt," I said and looked at Morten, who was trying to teach Victor to snorkel.

"What was that?"

"Nothing. Just me thinking out loud. Well, I'm glad you called and told me all this, officer. And I'm glad that it is all over. Let me know if there is anything more you need."

"I believe we can call this case closed now and move on. Have a nice trip home," he said. "I do hope you'll give our beautiful country another try one day. It truly has a lot more to offer than what you got to experience."

I laughed. "Of course I will. Thank you."

"Goodbye."

I hung up and sat for a little while, staring at my boyfriend and son trying to put on a snorkel. It seemed like Victor was getting used to having Morten around. It was good to know that they liked each other.

Christoffer was already in the water when Morten and Victor walked out to him and got in. I watched their snorkels move around in the water and chuckled. Victor seemed to like it. He stayed in for a long time. I stayed in the shade and went on Facebook to check on Maya. No new updates for two days now. I was sad that there were no new pictures or anything. I was worried about her. I didn't know what it was, but I had this feeling of unease inside of me. Like she needed me or something.

No, it was probably just me thinking my baby still needed me. I was a mother. It was only natural to think this, right? To be worried when your baby wasn't with you. To think they couldn't take care of themselves when you weren't around.

Of course it was. I was just being silly.

Christoffer had found something in the water and held it up in the air. My mom and dad clapped their hands when he ran to show them. I smiled. It was a nice ending to a terrible vacation after all. The next day, we would fly home and that would be it. It was over. I had spoken to Sophia and told her everything and, luckily, she wasn't angry with me at all. No, she was relieved that Christoffer was alright.

"I'm so sorry I put your son in danger," I said.

"Are you kidding me?" she answered. "I know you did everything you could. Heck, if it wasn't for you, he probably wouldn't be alive at all. I know I owe you one for this."

It was the best reaction I could have hoped for. I was so relieved.

I drew in a deep breath, then looked at my phone again, when it suddenly rang. I jumped when I saw who it was.

"Maya?" I said and took it.

"Hi, Mom."

Uh-oh. Something is wrong. I can hear it in her voice. Something is terribly wrong.

"What's going on, sweetheart?" I asked.

"Well...I was just wondering...I just wanted to..."

"Maya, what's wrong? I can hear it in your voice. Something is wrong."

Maya started sobbing.

"Maya, sweetheart. Just tell me. It's gonna be alright. I promise you."

"No," she cried. "No, it won't. Not this time, Mom."

"What on earth happened?"

"I...I...I got mad at Dad and stole his car..."

"You did what? Where are you Maya?"

"Wait. There's more."

I took in a deep breath to calm myself down. "Okay."

"I...oh, it's awful, Mom."

"Just tell me what it is. I won't get mad. Just tell me."

"Well...I...I...I kind of hit someone with it. It wasn't my fault, Mom. You have to believe me. Someone jumped right out in front of the car. There was nothing I could do."

"You hit someone? Who? What? Is he dead? Maya, you don't even have a license! Is this person alive?"

"I don't know. I don't dare to look. There's blood, Mom. There was blood on the windshield. Oh my God, Mom. I'm scared. What if I killed someone?"

"Well, where is the person now?"

"Still lying in the road in front of my car. Oh God, Mom. What if this person dies? Oh, Mom, please." Maya was crying loudly now.

"Easy, Maya. Calm down. Now, just take it easy, will you? I'm sure it'll be fine. Now I want you to hang up, then call 112 and talk to the police and have them send an ambulance. Then, you call your Dad."

"I can't do that, Mom. He'll kill me."

"But you have to. You need someone to be there with you. The police will take you in for questioning. Dad needs to be there. I'll be back tomorrow, then I'll come for you."

Maya went quiet. "You don't think Dad will kill me?"

"No. Don't be silly."

"He's been really mad lately, Mom. I'm scared of him. He yells at Victoria constantly. I even saw him hit her once. Mom, do you think he'll hit me?"

"If he does, I'll kill him. But he's your only chance now, Maya. Just call him, will you? Then call me back so I know you're safe. But first, call for an ambulance."

"Okay," Maya said with a very weak voice.

"Talk to you in a few minutes," I said. "I'll wait by the phone."

"Okay."

Two hours later, I still hadn't heard from her. I called her dad again and again, but got no answer. When he finally picked up, he told me he hadn't heard from her either. He had no idea what had happened. I had to tell him everything.

"I'm gonna kill her when I find her," Michael hissed angrily into the phone. "She's been nothing but a pain in the butt since she got here. Now, she stole my car? And wrecked it? I'm gonna kill her!"

It was while listening to him yell and hiss that I finally understood what Maya had tried to tell me. That was when I realized that she had tried to run away. And now she had done it again. This time, not just from her dad, but from both of us. And, worst of all, she had run from the consequences of her actions.

The End

———

Want to know what happens next? Get the next novel in the Emma Frost Mystery series here: Easy as One, Two, Three

AFTERWORD

Dear Reader,

Thank you for purchasing *Tweedledum and Tweedledee*. I know this one ends on a terrible cliffhanger, but I also assure you that you'll get a lot more of this part of the story in the next novel, where Emma starts the search for her runaway teenage daughter.

I truly hope you enjoyed this book. Don't forget to check out my other books if you haven't already read them. Just follow the links below. And don't forget to leave reviews, if you can.

Take care,
Willow

ABOUT THE AUTHOR

The Queen of Scream aka Willow Rose is a #1 Amazon Best-selling Author and an Amazon ALL-star Author of more than 80 novels. She writes Mystery, Paranormal, Romance, Suspense, Horror, Supernatural thrillers, and Fantasy.

Willow's books are fast-paced, nail-biting page-turners with twists you won't see coming.

Several of her books have reached the Kindle top 20 of ALL books in the US, UK, and Canada.

She has sold more than six million books all over the world.

Willow lives on Florida's Space Coast with her husband and two daughters. When she is not writing or reading, you will find her surfing and watch the dolphins play in the waves of the Atlantic Ocean.

Cover design by Juan Villar Padron,
https://juanjjpadron.wixsite.com/juanpadron

Special thanks to my editor Janell Parque
http://janellparque.blogspot.com/

———

Lightning Source UK Ltd.
Milton Keynes UK
UKHW041857190121
377353UK00012B/736/J